Oxford excellence for the Caribbean

Workbook 2

Oxford Mathematics for the Caribbean

CW00524809

Skills Workbook

Nicholas Goldberg

OXFORD
UNIVERSITY PRESS

OXFORD
UNIVERSITY PRESS

Great Clarendon Street, Oxford OX2 6DP

Oxford University Press is a department of the University of Oxford.
It furthers the University's objective of excellence in research,
scholarship, and education by publishing worldwide in

Oxford   New York

Auckland   Cape Town   Dar es Salaam   Hong Kong   Karachi
Kuala Lumpur   Madrid   Melbourne   Mexico City   Nairobi
New Delhi   Shanghai   Taipei   Toronto

With offices in

Argentina   Austria   Brazil   Chile   Czech Republic   France   Greece
Guatemala   Hungary   Italy   Japan   Poland   Portugal   Singapore
South Korea   Switzerland   Thailand   Turkey   Ukraine   Vietnam

Oxford is a registered trade mark of Oxford University Press
in the UK and in certain other countries

© Oxford University Press 2019

The moral rights of the author have been asserted

Database right Oxford University Press (maker)

First published 2019

All rights reserved. No part of this publication may be reproduced,
stored in a retrieval system, or transmitted, in any form or by any means,
without the prior permission in writing of Oxford University Press, or as
expressly permitted by law, or under terms agreed with the appropriate
reprographics rights organization. Enquiries concerning reproduction
outside the scope of the above should be sent to the Rights Department,
Oxford University Press, at the address above

You must not circulate this book in any other binding or cover
and you must impose this same condition on any acquirer

British Library Cataloguing in Publication Data

Data available

ISBN: 978-0-19-842577-9
10 9 8 7 6 5 4

Printed in Great Britain by Bell and Bain Ltd, Glasgow

MIX
Paper from
responsible sources
FSC   FSC® C007785
www.fsc.org

Contents

Introduction

This new **Oxford Maths for the Caribbean Workbook** accompanies the Student Textbook, providing additional mathematics support for students. Each chapter is matched to the Student Textbook to reinforce the concepts learned in class, and write-in pages offer instant practice.

You will find:

- a **wealth of questions** per topic, levelled in difficulty, with space for working-out and answers

- more **difficult questions**, indicated by an asterisk (*) to challenge more able students

- four **multiple choice** exercises, consolidating the topics covered throughout the book, allowing further opportunities to test understanding

- **hint boxes**, included as a reminder of key concepts introduced in the Student Textbook and in class

- numerical **answers** at the end of the book for reference

- **"I can do this!"** tick boxes on each page and a checklist at the end of the book, allowing students and teachers to track progress.

Each of these features has been incorporated to provide a comprehensive, reliable and easy-to-use resource for students, helping to boost skills and confidence, and improve grades.

Number

1.1 Reviewing fractions

1 What fraction of each shape is shaded?

(a)
(b)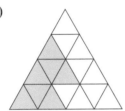
(c)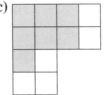
(d)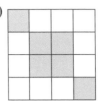

I can do
this page!

_____   _____   _____   _____

2 Complete:

(a) $\dfrac{2}{3} = \dfrac{}{15}$

(b) $\dfrac{3}{4} = \dfrac{}{24}$

(c) $\dfrac{5}{8} = \dfrac{}{32}$

(d) $\dfrac{3}{7} = \dfrac{}{35}$

(e) $\dfrac{1}{16} = \dfrac{}{80}$

(f) $\dfrac{7}{8} = \dfrac{}{72}$

(g) $\dfrac{5}{6} = \dfrac{}{78}$

(h) $\dfrac{5}{17} = \dfrac{}{102}$

3 Simplify these fractions. The first has been done for you.

(a) $\dfrac{15}{18} = \dfrac{\cancel{15}^{5}}{\cancel{18}_{6}} = \dfrac{5}{6}$

(b) $\dfrac{18}{21} =$

(c) $\dfrac{16}{24} =$

(d) $\dfrac{35}{80} =$

(e)* $\dfrac{26}{156} =$

(f)* $\dfrac{57}{133} =$

4 Write as improper fractions:

(a) $2\dfrac{1}{2} =$

(b) $3\dfrac{2}{3} =$

(c) $3\dfrac{7}{8} =$

(d) $5\dfrac{2}{5} =$

(e) $7\dfrac{9}{10} =$

(f) $4\dfrac{5}{16} =$

5 Write these improper fractions as mixed numbers:

(a) $\dfrac{18}{7} =$

(b) $\dfrac{33}{4} =$

(c) $\dfrac{16}{5} =$

(d) $\dfrac{38}{7} =$

(e) $\dfrac{47}{5} =$

(f) $\dfrac{63}{4} =$

6 Work out:

(a) $\dfrac{7}{8} + \dfrac{3}{8} =$

(b) $\dfrac{5}{9} + \dfrac{8}{9} =$

(c) $\dfrac{2}{3} + \dfrac{2}{3} + \dfrac{2}{3} + \dfrac{2}{3} =$

(d) $\dfrac{4}{5} + \dfrac{3}{5} + \dfrac{2}{5} + \dfrac{1}{5} =$

1.2 Adding and subtracting fractions

1 Complete:

(a) $\dfrac{3}{5} + \dfrac{3}{10} = \dfrac{6}{10} + \dfrac{3}{10} =$

(b) $\dfrac{3}{4} + \dfrac{3}{8} = \dfrac{}{8} + \dfrac{}{8} =$

(c) $\dfrac{5}{7} + \dfrac{2}{3} =$

(d) $\dfrac{6}{11} + \dfrac{3}{4} =$

(e) $\dfrac{4}{9} + \dfrac{5}{12} =$

(f) $\dfrac{6}{13} + \dfrac{15}{39} =$

(g) $\dfrac{2}{5} + \dfrac{19}{30} =$

(h) $\dfrac{8}{15} + \dfrac{19}{25} =$

I can do this page!

2 Work out these additions. The first one has been done for you.

(a) $3\dfrac{2}{3} + 2\dfrac{7}{8} = 5 + \dfrac{2}{3} + \dfrac{7}{8} = 5 + \dfrac{16}{24} + \dfrac{21}{24} = 5\dfrac{37}{24} = 6\dfrac{13}{34}$

(b) $2\dfrac{3}{4} + 3\dfrac{1}{3} =$

(c) $4\dfrac{1}{2} + 2\dfrac{7}{8} =$

(d) $1\dfrac{6}{7} + 2\dfrac{4}{5} =$

(e) $3\dfrac{1}{2} + 2\dfrac{3}{4} + 1\dfrac{7}{8} =$

3 Complete:

(a) $\dfrac{7}{8} - \dfrac{3}{4} = \dfrac{7}{8} - \dfrac{6}{8} =$

(b) $\dfrac{4}{5} - \dfrac{3}{10} =$

(c) $\dfrac{4}{7} - \dfrac{11}{21} =$

(d) $\dfrac{3}{8} - \dfrac{7}{24} =$

(e) $\dfrac{5}{9} - \dfrac{2}{7} =$

(f) $\dfrac{3}{4} - \dfrac{4}{11} =$

(g) $\dfrac{5}{13} - \dfrac{3}{8} =$

(h) $\dfrac{4}{9} - \dfrac{3}{17} =$

4 Jacky's school is $7\dfrac{1}{2}$ km from her home. If she walks $\dfrac{7}{8}$ km to the bus stop, how far does she travel on the bus?

_____ km

5* Marlon has $2\dfrac{1}{4}$ gallons of paint. He uses $1\dfrac{2}{3}$ gallons to paint a room.

(a) How much paint does he have left?

_____

(b) How much paint would he need for three such rooms?

_____

1.3 Multiplying and dividing fractions

1 Use the diagrams to complete the calculations shown.

I can do
this page!

(a) 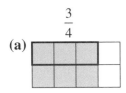   (b) 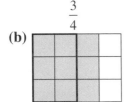   (c) 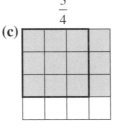   (d)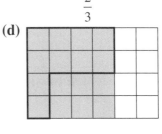

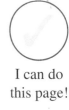

$\dfrac{1}{2}$ of $\dfrac{3}{4}$ = _____

$\dfrac{2}{3}$ of $\dfrac{3}{4}$ = _____

$\dfrac{3}{4}$ of $\dfrac{3}{4}$ = _____

$\dfrac{5}{8}$ of $\dfrac{2}{3}$ = _____

2 Complete:

(a) $\dfrac{3}{4} \times \dfrac{4}{9} = \dfrac{\cancel{3}^1}{\cancel{4}_1} \times \dfrac{\cancel{4}^1}{\cancel{9}_3} =$

(b) $\dfrac{2}{5} \times \dfrac{5}{12} =$

(c) $\dfrac{2}{3} \times \dfrac{3}{8} =$

(d) $\dfrac{4}{15} \times \dfrac{7}{8} =$

(e) $\dfrac{6}{7} \times \dfrac{2}{9} =$

(f) $\dfrac{8}{25} \times \dfrac{15}{32} =$

(g) $\dfrac{13}{20} \times \dfrac{15}{52} =$

(h) $\dfrac{6}{19} \times \dfrac{7}{42} =$

3 Work out the following. The first one has been done for you.

(a) $2\dfrac{3}{4} \times 1\dfrac{2}{5} = \dfrac{11}{4} \times \dfrac{7}{5} = \dfrac{77}{20} = 3\dfrac{17}{20}$

(b) $2\dfrac{7}{8} \times 2\dfrac{3}{5} =$

(c) $2\dfrac{1}{2} \times 6\dfrac{1}{4} =$

(d) $4\dfrac{2}{3} \times 5\dfrac{3}{5} =$

(e) $3\dfrac{2}{3} \times 4\dfrac{2}{3} =$

4 Use the diagrams to calculate the divisions shown.

(a) 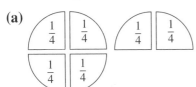   (b) 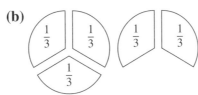   (c)

$1\dfrac{1}{2} \div \dfrac{1}{4} =$ _____

$1\dfrac{2}{3} \div \dfrac{1}{3} =$ _____

$\dfrac{1}{4} \div \dfrac{1}{8} =$ _____

5 Draw diagrams to show:

    (a) $2 \vee \frac{1}{4}$ **(b)** $3 \vee \frac{3}{4}$

I can do
this page!

6 Complete these divisions of fractions:

    (a) $\frac{2}{3} \div \frac{5}{18} = \frac{2}{\cancel{3}_1} \times \frac{\cancel{18}^6}{5} = \frac{12}{5} =$ **(b)** $\frac{3}{4} \div \frac{3}{10} =$

    (c) $\frac{3}{5} \div \frac{7}{15} =$ **(d)** $\frac{6}{11} \div \frac{8}{33} =$

    (e) $\frac{7}{8} \div \frac{3}{4} =$ **(f)** $\frac{4}{15} \div \frac{4}{5} =$

    (g) $\frac{6}{7} \div \frac{4}{21} =$ **(h)** $\frac{2}{15} \div \frac{8}{35} =$

> ### Remember
>
> To divide by a fraction, you turn the fraction over and multiply, e.g.
>
> $\div 3$ is the same as $\times \frac{1}{3}$
>
> $\div \frac{3}{4}$ is the same as $\times \frac{4}{3}$

7 Work out the following. The first one has been done for you.

    (a) $2\frac{3}{8} \div 1\frac{3}{4} = \frac{19}{8} \div \frac{7}{4} = \frac{19}{8} \times \frac{4}{7} = \frac{19}{\cancel{8}_2} \times \frac{\cancel{4}^1}{7} = \frac{19}{14} = 1\frac{5}{14}$

    (b) $2\frac{1}{2} \div 1\frac{2}{3} =$ **(c)** $3\frac{2}{3} \div 1\frac{1}{2} =$

    (d) $4\frac{3}{5} \div 2\frac{3}{8} =$ **(e)** $6\frac{5}{6} \div 3\frac{2}{3} =$

8 Panman had $6\frac{1}{2}$ bags of yams. He sold 5 bags. What fraction did he sell?

                                           _____

9 A race track is $\frac{2}{3}$ km long.

    (a) Curtley runs $5\frac{1}{2}$ laps of the track. How far does he run?

                                           _____

    (b) How many laps must he run to cover 10 km?

                                           _____

10* How many $8\frac{2}{3}$ cm pieces of cord can be cut from a ball of cord 160 cm long?

                                           _____

1.4 Ratio and proportion

1 Write the ratios in their simplest form.

I can do
this page!

(a) 40 : 8 = _____   **(b)** 25 : 65 = _____   **(c)** 60 : 15 = _____

(d) 28 : 84 = _____   **(e)** 68 : 51 = _____   **(f)** 128 : 144 = _____

2 Share $120 between James and John in the ratio.

(a) 3 : 1   **(b)** 5 : 3

(c) 3 : 7   **(d)** 19 : 5

3 The ratio of boys to girls at a school is 2 : 3. How many boys are there at the school if the number of girls is:

(a) 240   **(b)** 414

(c) 285?

4 Share:

(a) $60 in the ratio 2 : 3 : 5

(b) $625 in the ratio 4 : 9 : 12

(c) 57 goats in the ratio 2 : 5 : 12

*5 Draw a line 15 cm long and divide it in the ratio:

(a) 1 : 2 : 2

(b) 1 : 2 : 3

*6 A sum of money is shared among Paula, Peggy and Princess in the ratio 2 : 3 : 7. How much does Paula receive if Princess gets $343?

1.5 Number bases

I can do
this page!

1 Complete the table to find the base 10 numbers represented by these binary numbers. The first one has been done for you.

2^5	2^4	2^3	2^2	2^1	2^0	Number
		1	0	1	0	$2^3 + 2^1 = 8 + 2 = 10$
		1	1	0	1	
	1	0	1	1	1	
1	0	1	0	1	0	
1	1	0	1	0	1	

2 Change these binary numbers to base 10.

(a) 1111 _____

(b) 10110 _____

(c) 101110 _____

(d) 1111110 _____

3 Change these base 10 numbers to base 2.

(a) 16 _____

(b) 12 _____

(c) 24 _____

(d) 30 _____

4 Complete the table to find the base 10 numbers represented by these base 5 numbers:

5^3	5^2	5^1	5^0	Number
	1	3	4	
	4	2	3	
3	0	4	4	
4	1	2	2	

5 Write these base 10 numbers in base 5.

(a) 12 _____

(b) 20 _____

(c) 26 _____

(d) 120 _____

6 Work out these base 5 calculations:

(a) $21 + 24$

(b) $413 - 34$

Decimals

2.1 Ordering decimals

1

Show these numbers on the number line:

(a) 0.6   **(b)** 2.2   **(c)** 1.55   **(d)** 2.95   **(e)** 0.05

✓

I can do
this page!

2 Estimate the value of the letters on this number line.

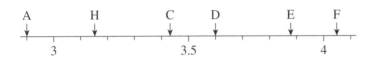

A =   B =   C =   D =   E =   F =

3 Identify the smallest number in each set.

(a) 6.4, 0.42, 0.073, 0.91, 5   _____

(b) 8, 0.084, 0.9, 0.09, 3.2   _____

(c) 0.303, 0.33, 0.41, 0.3, 3   _____

4 Write down three numbers that lie between

(a) 3.4 and 3.5   _____, _____, _____

(b) 0.61 and 0.63   _____, _____, _____

(c) 0.09 and 0.1   _____, _____, _____

5 Use your ruler to draw lines with length

(a) 5.2 cm

(b) 0.7 cm

(c) 6.0 cm

6 The heights, in metres, of four boys were

     1.6   2   1.78   1.82

(a) Who was the tallest?

_____

(b) How much taller was the tallest boy than the next tallest boy?

_____

2.2 Adding and subtracting decimals

I can do
this page!

1 Work out

(a)   8
        14.68
     + 7.04
     ───────

(b)   0.07
        3.2
     + 1.94
     ───────

(c) 143
      61.72
     + 9.8
     ───────

(d)   0.3
       10.71
     + 0.043
     ───────

2 Work out

(a) $17 - 2.64 =$ _____

     17
   − 2.64
   ───────

(b) $3.1 - 1.68 =$ _____

(c) $183 - 0.647 =$ _____

3 Deshane is 2 m tall. How much taller is he than his brother Jomo who is 1.76 m?

_____

4 In 2003, Usain Bolt took first place in the World Youth Championships 200 m race
with a time of 20.4 s. How much slower was this than his world record time of 19.19 s?

_____

5 The masses of four eggs in grams were

49, 53.62, 60.1, 43.09

(a) What was their total mass?

_____

(b) What was the mass of a fifth egg if the new total mass was 250 g?

_____

6 Complete:

(a) $63.4 -$ ☐ $= 18.65$

(b) $2 + 19.48 +$ ☐ $= 154$

(c) ☐ $- 1.063 = 6.94$

2.3 Multiplying and dividing decimals 1

1 **Without** using your calculator, work out:

I can do
this page!

(a) $3.6 \times 10 =$

(b) $17.4 \times 100 =$

(c) $68 \div 10 =$

(d) $342 \div 1000 =$

(e) $1.13 \times 1000 =$

(f) $49.5 \div 100 =$

(g) $0.042 \times 100 =$

(h) $8.03 \div 10 =$

(i) $6.06 \times 100 =$

2 Complete:

(a) $56 \div \boxed{} = 0.056$

(b) $0.062 \times \boxed{} = 6.2$

(c) $\boxed{} \times 0.73 = 730$

(d) $\boxed{} \div 100 = 7.895$

(e) $\boxed{} \times 10 = 0.73$

(f) $\boxed{} \div 100 = 9.52$

3 Given that $34 \times 76 = 2586$, work out:

(a) $3.4 \times 7.6 =$ _____

(b) $3.4 \times 76 =$ _____

(c) $0.34 \times 7.6 =$ _____

(d) $0.034 \times 76 =$ _____

(e) 0.34×0.76 _____

(f) $340 \times 0.76 =$ _____

4 Work out:

(a) $\begin{array}{r} 2.3 \\ \times\, 3.6 \\ \hline \end{array}$

(b) $\begin{array}{r} 0.37 \\ \times\, 8.4 \\ \hline \end{array}$

(c) $\begin{array}{r} 42.3 \\ \times\, 3.2 \\ \hline \end{array}$

(d) $\begin{array}{r} 6.48 \\ \times\, 0.07 \\ \hline \end{array}$

2.4 Multiplying and dividing decimals 2

I can do
this page!

1 Work out the following. The first one has been done for you.

(a) $0.092 \div 4$

$$
\begin{array}{r}
0.023 \\
4\overline{)0.09^{1}2}
\end{array}
$$

(b) $4.24 \div 4$

$$
\begin{array}{r}
 \\
4\overline{)4.24}
\end{array}
$$

(c) $31.25 \div 5$

$$
\begin{array}{r}
 \\
5\overline{)31.25}
\end{array}
$$

(d) $0.064 \div 8$

(e) $4.347 \div 9$

(f) $0.4734 \div 6$

2 (a) Six jerk chicken 'specials' were sold in a restaurant for $80.52.
What is the cost of one special?

_____

(b) What is the cost of 13 specials?

_____

3 Complete these divisions. The first one has been done for you.

(a) $0.471 \div 0.06 = \underline{7.85}$

$$\frac{0.471}{0.06} = \frac{0.471 \times 100}{0.06 \times 100} = \frac{47.1}{6} = 7.85$$

(b) $16.4 \div 0.04 = $ _____

$$\frac{16.4}{0.04} =$$

(c) $3.75 \div 0.5 = $ _____

$$\frac{3.75}{0.5} =$$

4* Jamaica's Hansle Parchment ran the 110 m hurdles in a time of 13.14 s.

(a) What is his speed in metres per second?

_____

(b) How far could he run at this speed in 6.47 s?

_____

2.5 Squares and square roots

1 Write down the squares of:

(a) 14 _____ (b) 17 _____ (c) 24 _____ (d) 87 _____

I can do
this page!

2 Write down the square roots of:

(a) 81 _____ (b) 729 _____ (c) 1296 _____ (d) 2704 _____

3 Complete the table.

Numbers between	Square numbers	Number of squares
100 and 199	100, 121, 144, 169, 194	5
200 and 299		
300 and 399		
400 and 499		
500 and 599		
600 and 699		

Remember

To **square** a number you multiply it by itself. The inverse of the square of a number is called its **square root** ($\sqrt{\ }$).

4 **Without** using the $\boxed{\sqrt{\ }}$ button on your calculator, complete the tables to find the square roots shown.

(a) $\sqrt{19}$

Guess	Guess squared	Result
4	16	too small
4.5	20.25	too big

(b) $\sqrt{42}$

Guess	Guess squared	Result
7	49	too big

5 What is the perimeter of a square that has an area of 1900 m^2?

_____

6* What is the smallest square number bigger than 10 000?

_____

2.6 Rounding numbers

1   Mark with the letter X each of the decimals shown on the number line.
Use the number line to round each to one decimal place.

I can do
this page!

(a) 1.37   **(b)** 2.53   **(c)** 17.86

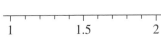

1.37 = _____ (1 d.p.)   2.53 = _____ (1 d.p.)   17.86 = _____ (1 d.p.)

2

```
|‑‑‑‑‑‑‑‑‑‑‑‑‑‑‑‑‑‑‑‑‑‑‑‑‑‑‑‑‑‑‑‑‑|
1          2          3          4
```

Use the number line to help you write the following to one decimal place.

(a) 1.64 _____   **(b)** 3.13 _____   **(c)** 2.84 _____

> ### Remember
>
> You can round off a decimal to
> a number of decimal places (d.p.)
> e.g. 24.6782 = 24.678 (3 d.p.)
>   = 24.68 (2 d.p.)
>   = 24.7 (1 d.p.)

(d) 3.19 _____   **(e)** 2.55 _____   **(f)** 1.26 _____

(g) 2.05 _____   **(h)** 1.09 _____   **(i)** 3.01 _____

3   Write the following numbers correct to two decimal places.

(a) 1.286 _____   **(b)** 6.913 _____   **(c)** 4.217 _____

(d) 8.918 _____   **(e)** 14.326 _____   **(f)** 0.028 _____

(g) 0.716 _____   **(h)** 0.208 _____   **(i)** 0.839 _____

4   Complete the table.

Decimal	Rounded to 1 d.p.	Rounded to 2 d.p.	Rounded to 3 d.p.
6.4152			
18.7943			
0.01762			
0.9927			
12.3847			

2.7 Significant figures

1

Use the number line to write these numbers to the nearest 10.

(a) 31 _____   (b) 56 _____   (c) 64 _____   (d) 69 _____

I can do
this page!

2 Write correct to one significant figure.

(a) 56 _____   (b) 64 _____   (c) 18 _____   (d) 9 _____

3 Complete the table.

Number	8245	2036	4893	11932	306469
to 3 sig. fig					
to 2 sig. fig					
to 1 sig. fig	8000				

4 Write to one significant figure.

(a) 4.3 _____   (b) 0.68 _____   (c) 0.0084 _____   (d) 17.61 _____

5 Complete the table.

Number	0.8462	0.01698	0.4164	0.008947	0.0006246
to 3 sig. fig					
to 2 sig. fig					
to 1 sig. fig	0.8				

6 Andrew's annual salary when written to one significant figure is $60000.
What is

(a) the maximum salary he could have earned?   _____

(b) the minimum salary he could have earned?   _____

7 Estimate the answer to these problems to one significant figure.

(a) 694×783 _____

(b) 0.0284×0.984 _____

(c) 3187.6×24.03 _____

2.8 Standard form

1 Copy and complete:

(a) $6000 = 6 \times \underline{\hspace{1cm}} = 6 \times 10^3$

(b) $890 = \underline{\hspace{1cm}} \times 100 = \underline{\hspace{1cm}} \times 10^2$

I can do this page!

(c) $4300 = \underline{\hspace{1cm}} \times 1000 = \underline{\hspace{1cm}} \times 10^3$

(d) $72 = \underline{\hspace{1cm}} \times 10 = \underline{\hspace{1cm}} \times 10^1$

(e) $29\,400 = \underline{\hspace{1cm}} \times 10\,000 = \underline{\hspace{1cm}} \times 10^5$

(f) $6934 = \underline{\hspace{1cm}} \times 1000 = \underline{\hspace{1cm}} \times 10^3$

2 Write these numbers in full:

(a) $3 \times 10^4 = 3 \times 10000 = \underline{\hspace{2cm}}$

(b) $3.7 \times 10^2 = \underline{\hspace{2cm}}$

(c) $1.85 \times 10^4 = \underline{\hspace{2cm}}$

(d) $2.8 \times 10^5 = \underline{\hspace{2cm}}$

(e) $7.68 \times 10^3 = \underline{\hspace{2cm}}$

(f) $4.09 \times 10^6 = \underline{\hspace{2cm}}$

3 Write in standard form:

(a) $9000 = \underline{\hspace{2cm}}$

(b) $7600 = \underline{\hspace{2cm}}$

(c) $890 = \underline{\hspace{2cm}}$

(d) $74 = \underline{\hspace{2cm}}$

(e) $1460 = \underline{\hspace{2cm}}$

(f) $33600 = \underline{\hspace{2cm}}$

(g) $81.6 = \underline{\hspace{2cm}}$

(h) $212.94 = \underline{\hspace{2cm}}$

(i) $603.61 = \underline{\hspace{2cm}}$

(j) $73\,604 = \underline{\hspace{2cm}}$

4 Write in order of size in ascending order:

(a) $63, 6 \times 10^2, 602, 5.98 \times 10, 4 \times 10^3$ _____

(b) $1.8 \times 10^4, 2000, 2.1 \times 10^3, 1.9 \times 10^3, 3164$ _____

5 In the 2011 census, the population of Jamaica was $2\,697\,983$.

(a) What is this in standard form?

(b) What was the population in 2001 if there are 9.0351×10^4 more people in 2011 than in 2001?

6 Find the exact value of $17.4 \times 28.9 - 6.3$, writing your answer in standard form.

2.9 Decimals and fractions

1 Write these decimals as fractions in their simplest form:

(a) 0.3 =

(b) 0.35 =

(c) 0.46 =

(d) 0.375 =

(e) 0.0625 =

(f) 0.4375 =

I can do
this page!

2 Change these fractions to decimals. The first one has been done for you.

(a) $\dfrac{7}{8} = 7 \div 8$ $8\overline{)7.{}^70{}^60{}^40}$ 0.875

(b) $\dfrac{5}{8} =$

(c) $\dfrac{4}{9} =$

(d) $\dfrac{5}{12} =$

(e) $\dfrac{5}{6} =$

Check your answers with a calculator.

3 Use your calculator to write these fractions as decimals correct to 3 decimal places.

(a) $\dfrac{2}{7} =$

(b) $\dfrac{5}{13} =$

(c) $\dfrac{11}{14} =$

(d) $\dfrac{4}{17} =$

(e) $\dfrac{12}{13} =$

(f) $\dfrac{3}{11} =$

4* Use your calculator to find fractions equivalent to these recurring decimals.

(a) 0.11111… =

(b) 0.090909… =

(c) 0.454545… =

(d) 0.41666… =

Angles

3.1 Measuring and drawing angles

1 Estimate, then measure each of these angles with your protractor

(a)

(b)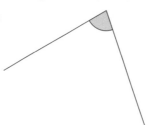

(c)

 I can do this page!

Estimate = _____   Estimate = _____   Estimate = _____

Actual = _____   Actual = _____   Actual = _____

2 Draw accurately using your protractor angles of:

(a) 40°   (b) 84°   (c) 163°

_____   _____   _____

3 Draw accurately the triangle XYZ where:

(a) XY = 6 cm, ZX̂Y = 43°, XŶZ = 26°   (b) XY = 5.6 cm, ZX̂Y = 34°, XŶZ = 34°

3.2 Constructions

1   Using a ruler and protractor, draw accurately the triangle PQR with:

(a) PQ = 7 cm, $\hat{P}$ = 34°, $\hat{Q}$ = 42°   (b) PQ = 8.5 cm, $\hat{P}$ = 58°, $\hat{Q}$ = 29°

I can do
this page!

2   Using a ruler and compass construct an angle of:

(a) 90° at the point X on the line PQ   (b) 60° at the point T on the line ST.

P   X   Q   S   T

3   Using a ruler and compass, bisect the angle:

(a) A$\hat{B}$C   (b) D$\hat{E}$F

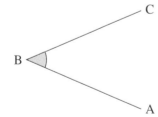

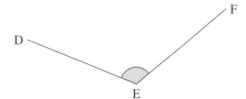

4 Construct an equilateral triangle, XYZ, with side XY = 7 cm, using a ruler and compass only.

I can do
this page!

5 **(a)** Construct the rectangle ABCD with AB = 12 cm and BC = 5 cm using a ruler and compass.

(b) Measure the diagonal AC = _____ cm

6 Using a ruler and compass, construct the triangle PQR, with
(a) PQ = 7.6 cm, $\hat{P} = 30°$ and $\hat{Q} = 60°$

(b) PQ = 6.9 cm, $\hat{P} = 90°, \hat{Q} = 45°$

3.3 Angles and lines

1 Find the size of the lettered angles.

(a)

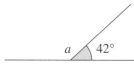

$a =$ _____

(b)

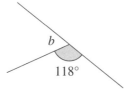

$b =$ _____

(c)

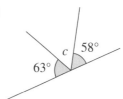

I can do
this page!

2 Calculate the value of the lettered angle.

(a)

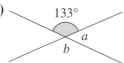

$a =$ _____ $b =$ _____

(b)

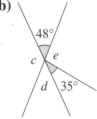

$c =$ _____ $d =$ _____

$e =$ _____

3 Find the angle marked by the letter.

(a)

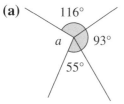

$a =$ _____

(b)

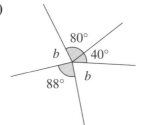

$b =$ _____

(c)

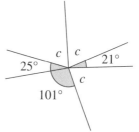

$c =$ _____

4 Find the value of the angle x in each diagram.

(a)

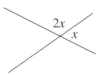

$x =$ _____

(b)

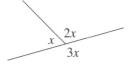

$x =$ _____

(c)

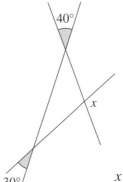

$x =$ _____

3.4 Angles in triangles and quadrilaterals

1 **(a)** Measure the interior angles of these triangles:

(i)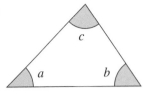

(ii)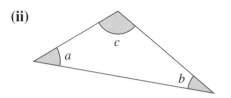

$a =$ _____ , $b =$ _____ , $c =$ _____ $a =$ _____ , $b =$ _____ , $c =$ _____

$a + b + c =$ _____ $a + b + c =$ _____

(b) What can you say about the sum of the interior angles in a triangle?

_____

2 Find the missing angles in these triangles:

(a)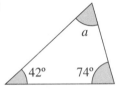

(b)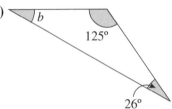

(c)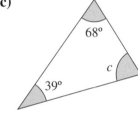

$a =$ _____ $b =$ _____ $c =$ _____

3 **(a)** Measure the interior angles of these quadrilaterals:

(i)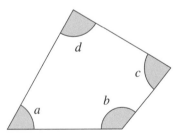

(ii)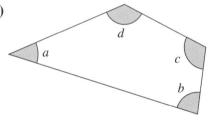

$a =$ ____ , $b =$ ____ , $c =$ ____ , $d =$ ____ $a =$ ____ , $b =$ ____ , $c =$ ____ , $d =$ ____

4 Find the missing angles in these quadrilaterals:

(a)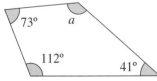

(b)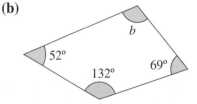

(c)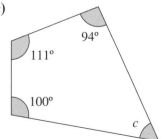

$a =$ _____ $b =$ _____ $c =$ _____

I can do
this page!

3.5 Parallel lines

1 **(a)** Use your protractor to measure these angles:

(i)

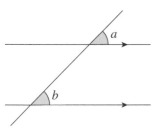

(ii)

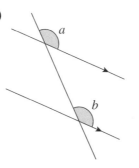

(iii)

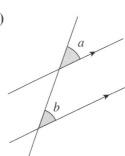

I can do
this page!

$a =$ _____, $b =$ _____ $a =$ _____, $b =$ _____ $a =$ _____, $b =$ _____

(b) Complete: Corresponding angles are _____

2 **(a)** Use your protractor to measure these angles:

(i)

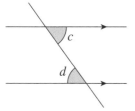

(ii)

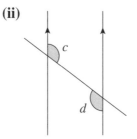

(iii)

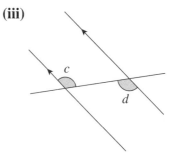

$c =$ _____, $d =$ _____ $c =$ _____, $d =$ _____ $c =$ _____, $d =$ _____

(b) Complete: Alternate angles are _____

3 Find the value of these missing angles: Give reasons for each of your answers

(a)

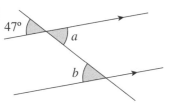

(b)

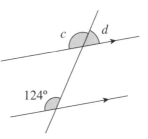

$a =$ _____ (vertically opposite) $c =$ _____ (   )

$b =$ _____ (   ) $d =$ _____ (   )

(c)

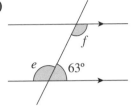

$e =$ _____ (   )

$f =$ _____ (   )

(d)

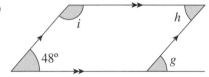

$g =$ _____ (   ) $h =$ _____ (   )

$i =$ _____ (   )

I can do
this page!

(e)

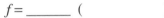

$j =$ _____ (   )

$k =$ _____ (   )

(f)

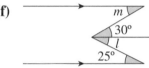

$l =$ _____ (   )

$m =$ _____ (   )

4   Calculate the lettered angles

(a)

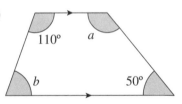

$a =$ _____, $b =$ _____

(b)

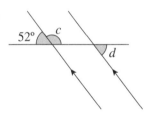

$c =$ _____, $d =$ _____

(c)

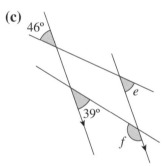

$e =$ _____, $f =$ _____

(d)

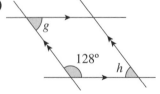

$g =$ _____, $i =$ _____

(e)

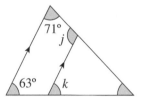

$j =$ _____, $k =$ _____

(f)

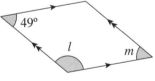

$l =$ _____, $m =$ _____

(g)

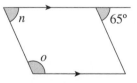

$n =$ _____, $o =$ _____

(h)

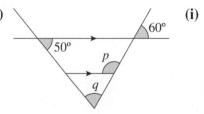

$p =$ _____, $q =$ _____

(i)

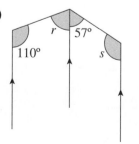

$r =$ _____, $s =$ _____

Multiple choice 1

In each question, circle the correct answer.

1 Which is the biggest fraction?

A $\frac{3}{4}$ B $\frac{5}{8}$ C $\frac{7}{11}$ D $\frac{9}{13}$

2 Newtown is $1\frac{1}{4}$ km south of Roseau, while

Canefield is $2\frac{5}{8}$ km north of Roseau. How far
is Newtown from Canefield?

A $1\frac{3}{8}$ km   B $3\frac{7}{16}$ km   C $3\frac{1}{2}$ km   D $3\frac{7}{8}$ km

3 How many $\frac{2}{3}$ kg bags of coffee beans can be
made from a 15 kg container of beans?

A 5   B 10   C 15   D $22\frac{1}{2}$

4 Jackson walks $2\frac{1}{2}$ km to work. He stops after
1 km to go into a shop. What fraction of the way
has he still to walk?

A $\frac{2}{5}$ B $\frac{3}{5}$ C $\frac{5}{3}$ D $\frac{5}{2}$

5 The sum of $140 is shared in the ration 3:7
between Loftus and Larry. How much does Loftus
receive?

A $42   B $60   C $80   D 98

6 A bag of limes weighs $1\frac{3}{8}$ kg. What is the weight
of 8 such bags?

A $8\frac{3}{8}$ kg   B $9\frac{3}{8}$ kg   C 11 kg   D 32 kg

7 The binary number 11011 is which decimal
number?

A 11   B 13   C 27   D 54

8 Kirani James of Grenada won the 2012 Olympic
400 m title in 43.94 s.
By how much did he beat the 45 s barrier?

A 1.06 s   B 1.94 s   C 2.06 s   D 2.94 s

9 What is the cost of 3.2 kg of pigeon
peas at $ 7.25 per kilogram?

A $2.32   B $3.52

C $23.20   D $35.25

I can do
this page!

10 How many 0.35-litre bottles of juice can be
filled from a bowl holding 7 litres of juice?

A 2   B 5   C 20   D 50

11 Johan Blake's best time for 100 m is 9.69 s.
What is this to one decimal place?

A 9.6 s   B 9.7 s   C 9.0 s   D 10.0 s

12 The number 35200 written in standard from is:

A 3.52×10^2 B 35.2×10^3

C 3.52×10^4 D 35.2×10^2

13 A square has area 400 m². What is the length
of its sides?

A 6.32 m   B 20 m   C 63.2 m   D 100 m

14 Andrew is 1.8 m tall. His sister is 1.64 m tall.
How much taller is Andrew?

A 0.14 m   B 0.16 m   C 0.24 m   D 2.44 m

15 What is 5960.8 written to 2 significant figures.

A 59   B 60   C 5900   D 6000

16

The angle shown is

A acute   B obtuse   C reflex   D right-angled

17

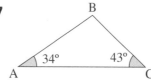

What is the angle A$\hat{B}$C?

A 13°   **B** 77°   **C** 103°   **D** 123°

In the diagram, *x* is

A 18°   **B** 62°

C 118°   **D** 152°

I can do
this page!

18

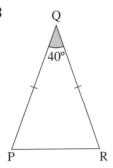

PQR is an isosceles triangle with PQ = QR.
What is the angle Q$\hat{P}$R if angle P$\hat{Q}$R = 40°?

A 20°   **B** 50°   **C** 70°   **D** 80°

19

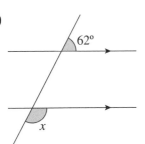

20

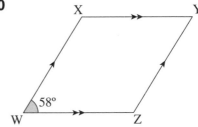

WXYZ is a parallelogram with angle X$\hat{W}$Z = 58°.
What is angle X$\hat{Y}$Z?

A 32°   **B** 58°   **C** 122°   **D** 128°

Check your answers in the back of the book:

Score = $\dfrac{}{20}$

Sets

4.1 Intersection of sets

1 **(a)**

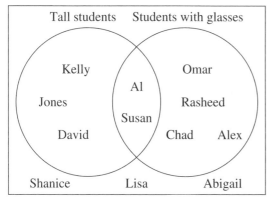

(b)

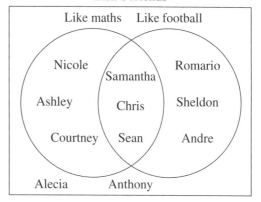

I can do this page!

From the Venn diagram, list the students who:

(i) are tall _____

(ii) have glasses _____

(iii) are tall and have glasses _____

From the Venn diagram, list the students who:

(i) like maths _____

(ii) like football _____

(iii) like maths and football _____

2 Complete:

(a) {1, 2, 3, 4, 5} ∩ {2, 4, 6, 8, 10} =

(b) {even numbers} ∩ {first 5 multiples of 7} =

(c) {odd numbers under 35} ∩ {multiples of 8} =

(d) {factors of 24} ∩ {factors of 32} =

(e) {factors of 60} ∩ {multiples of 3} =

3* **(a)** Draw Venn diagrams to show these sets:

U = {whole numbers 1 to 15}

A = {3, 7, 11, 15}

B = {4, 5, 6, 7, 8, 9, 10, 11}

Whole numbers 1–15

(b) What is A ∩ B?

_____

4.2 Union of sets

I can do
this page!

1 Complete:

(a) {2, 4, 6, 8} ∪ {1, 2, 3, 4} =

(b) {6, 16, 26, 36, 46} ∪ {4, 14} =

(c) {a, d, c, d, e, f, g} ∪ {b, d, f} =

(d) {factors of 10} ∪ {factors of 8} =

(e) {first 5 multiples of 4} ∪ {factors of 16} =

2 Complete these Venn diagrams:

(a)

Whole numbers 1–20

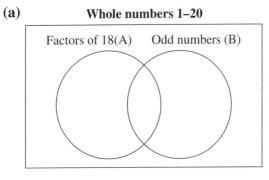

Factors of 18(A)   Odd numbers (B)

List

(i) A ∪ B =   (ii) A ∩ B =

(b)

Whole numbers 1–30

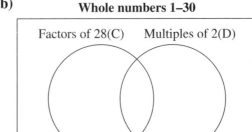

Factors of 28(C)   Multiples of 2(D)

List

(i) C ∪ D =   (ii) C ∩ D =

3 Given U = {whole numbers 1–30}, draw Venn diagrams to show:

(a) (i) A = {factors of 36}

       B = {factors of 18}

Whole numbers 1–30

(ii) What is A ∪ B? _____

(b) (i) C = {first seven multiples of 4}

       D = {first 15 multiples of 2}

Whole numbers 1–30

(ii) What is C ∪ D? _____

4 In the Venn diagrams, shade A ∪ B.

(a)

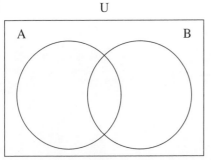

(b)

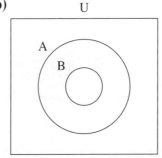

(c)

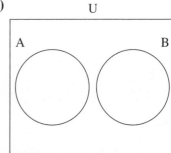

4.3 Complements of a set

Remember

Where A is a subset of the universal set U, the **complement** of A contains the members of U that are *not* in A. The symbol for the complement of A is A′.

I can do this page!

1 U = {whole numbers 1 to 20}. Find the complement of A in each of the following cases.

(a) A = {2, 4, 6, 8, 10, 12, 14}, A′ = {   }

(b) A = {factors of 18}, A′ =

(c) A = {first five multiples of 4}, A′ =

(d) A = {composite numbers to 20}, A′ =

(e) A = {whole numbers 2–16}, A′ =

2 Describe the complement of each of these subsets.

(a)
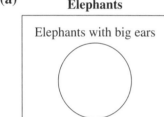

(b)
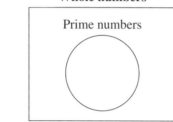

(c)
Coffee beans

Blue Mountain coffee beans

_____   _____   _____

3 Using the Venn diagrams, describe the following sets.

(a)
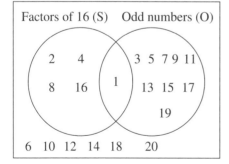

(i) S′ =

(ii) O′ =

(iii) S′ ∪ O′ =

(b)
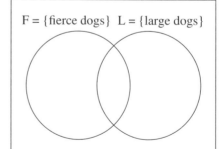

(i) F ∩ L =

(ii) F′ =

(iii) (F ∩ L)′ =

Measurement

(5)

5.1 Metric units

1 What metric unit would you use to measure

(a) the distance of your home from New York   _____

(b) the mass of an exercise book   _____

(c) the length of your toenails   _____

(d) the mass of a giraffe   _____

(e) the distance around your neck?   _____

I can do
this page!

2 Write down three things that have:

(a) a length of approximately 5 mm

_____

_____

_____

(b) a mass of approximately 5 grams

_____

_____

_____

3 Complete these tables:

(a)

Centimetres	Metres	Kilometres
	5	
	2 × 1000 =	2
15 × 100	15	
		0.04
	17.3	

(b)

Grams	Kilograms
160	
6 × 1000 =	6
	2.1
8134	
	0.042

4 Given 1 inch = 2.54 cm and 1 kg = 2.2 lb, complete the tables.

(a) Distance

Centimetres	Inches
	12
50	
	3
280	
	$5\frac{1}{2}$

(b) Mass

Pounds (lb)	Kilograms (kg)
	5
8	
	14
$4\frac{1}{2}$	
	6.8

5.2 Perimeter

1 Find the perimeter of each shape.

(a)

4 cm

6 cm

$p =$ _____

(b)

6 cm   5.5 cm

5 cm

$p =$ _____

(c)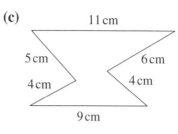

11 cm

5 cm   6 cm

4 cm   4 cm

9 cm

$p =$ _____

 I can do this page!

Remember

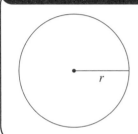

r

The **circumference** of a circle, C, is given by

$C = 2\pi r$

where r = radius of circle and $\pi = 3.14$

---

2 Find the circumference of a circle with radius:

(a) 5 cm

$C =$

(b) 8.4 cm

$C =$

3 Find the diameter of a circle with circumference:

(a) 42 cm

$D =$

(b) 5.4 cm

$D =$

4* Find the perimeter of these shapes. Take $\pi = 3.14$

(a)

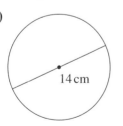

14 cm

$p =$ _____

(b) ←——— 9 cm ———→

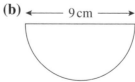

$p =$ _____

(c) ←——8 cm——→

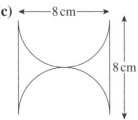

8 cm

$p =$ _____

(d)

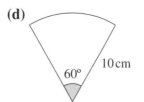

60°   10 cm

$p =$ _____

5.3 Areas of triangles and parallelograms

1 Find the area of these rectangles:

(a)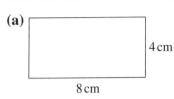

4 cm

8 cm

Area =

(b)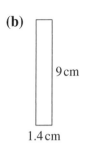

9 cm

1.4 cm

Area =

(c)

6.4 cm

6.4 cm

Area =

I can do
this page!

2 Find the areas of these triangles. The first one has been done for you.

(a)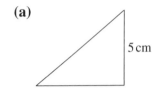

5 cm

6 cm

Area $= \dfrac{1}{2} \times 6\,\text{cm} \times 5\,\text{cm} = 15\,\text{cm}^2$

(b)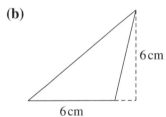

6 cm

6 cm

Area =

(c)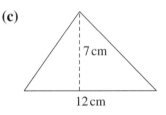

7 cm

12 cm

Area =

3 Find the area of these parallelograms. The first one has been done for you.

(a)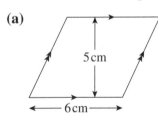

5 cm

6 cm

Area = b × h = 6 cm × 5 cm

= 30 cm²

(b)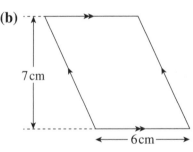

7 cm

6 cm

Area = _____

(c)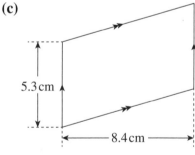

5.3 cm

8.4 cm

Area = _____

4 A right-angled triangle has base length 9 cm. What is its perpendicular height if the triangle has an area of 36 cm²?

_____

5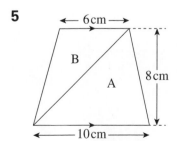

6 cm

B

A

8 cm

10 cm

In the diagrams find the area of:

(a) triangle A   _____

(b) triangle B   _____

(c) the whole shape   _____

6 Find the area of each of the lettered shapes:

(a)

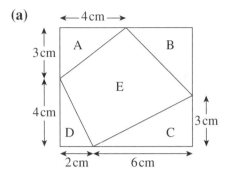

A = _____   B = _____

C = _____   D = _____

E = _____

(b)

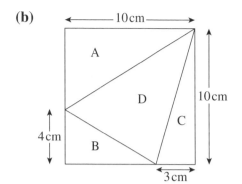

A = _____   B = _____

C = _____   D = _____

I can do
this page!

7* Find the area of these composite shapes:

(a)

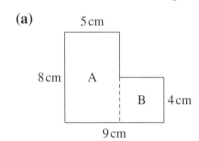

Area A =

Area B =

Total area =

(b)

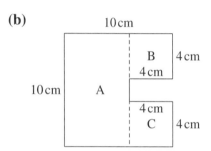

Area A =

Area B =

Area C =   Total area =

(c)

Area A =

Area B =

Total area =

(d)

4 cm

6 cm

11 cm

Total area =

(e)

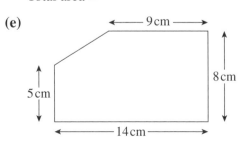

Total area =

5.4 Area of a circle

1 **(a)** Find the area of these circles by counting squares.

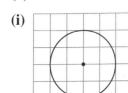

(i)   **(ii)**   **(iii)**   **(iv)**   I can do this page!

Area = _____   Area = _____   Area = _____   Area = _____

(b) Complete the table.

Circle	Area	Radius, r (units)	r^2	$3.14 \times r^2$
i		2	4	
ii				
iii				
iv				

Remember

The area of a circle, A, is given by $A = \pi r^2$ where $\pi = 3.14$

(c) What do you notice about columns 2 and 5 of the table?

_____

2 Using $\pi = 3.14$, find the area, A, of these circles.

(a)   **(b)**    **(c)** 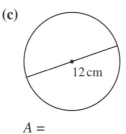   **(d)**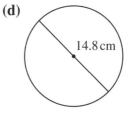

5 cm   7.2 cm   12 cm   14.8 cm

$A = \pi r^2$ $A =$ $A =$ $A =$

$= 3.14 \times 5^2 \, \text{cm}$

$=$

3 Using $\pi = 3.14$, find the area, A, of these shapes.

(a) 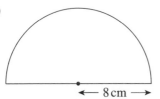   **(b)**   **(c)**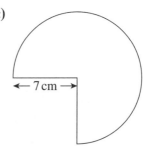

← 8 cm →   ←4.5 cm→   ← 7 cm →

$A =$ _____ $A =$ _____ $A =$ _____

5.5 Scale drawings

1 A small rectangular room is 4 m long and 3 m wide.
Make a scale drawing of the room using the scales given below.

(a) 1 cm represents 1 m

(b) 1 cm represents 2 m

I can do
this page!

2 The map shows Dominica.

Dominica

Portsmouth

Marigot

La Plaine

Roseau

Grand Bay

(a) On the map how far is it in centimetres from

(i) Roseau to Portsmouth _____

(ii) Portsmouth to La Plaine _____

(iii) Grand Bay to Marigot? _____

(b) What is the actual distance in kilometres from

(i) Roseau to Portsmouth _____

(ii) Portsmouth to La Plaine _____

(iii) Grand Bay to Marigot? _____

Scale 1 cm represents 6 km

3 Write these scales in ratio form. The first one has been done for you.

(a) 1 cm represents 2 m = 1:2 × 100
= 1:200

(b) 1 cm represents 5 m =

(c) 1 cm represents 2 km =

(d) 1 mm represents 4 km =

4 Complete the table.

Distance on map	Scale	Actual distance
5 cm	1:10 000	5 × 10 000 cm = _____ km
4 km ÷ 20 000 = _____ cm	1:20 000	4 km
7.5 cm	1:100 000	
	1:50 000	25 km
14.4 cm	1:800 000	

Integers

6.1 Adding integers

Remember

When you add a negative number you move to the left on the number line.
For example:

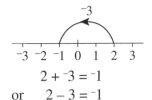

$$2 + {}^-3 = {}^-1$$
or $\quad 2 - 3 = {}^-1$

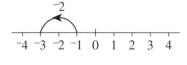

$${}^-1 + {}^-2 = {}^-3$$
or $\quad {}^-1 - 2 = {}^-3$

I can do
this page!

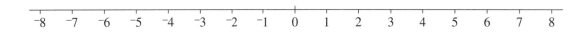

1 Use the number line to help you work out:

(a) $2 + {}^-4 =$ _____

(b) $3 + {}^-4 =$ _____

(c) $4 + {}^-4 =$ _____

(d) $5 + {}^-2 =$ _____

(e) ${}^-5 + {}^-2 =$ _____

(f) ${}^-6 + {}^-2 =$ _____

(g) ${}^-3 + {}^-2 =$ _____

(h) $4 + {}^-1 =$ _____

(i) $8 + {}^-12 =$ _____

2 Work out:

(a) ${}^-5 - 4 =$ _____

(b) ${}^-3 + 5 =$ _____

(c) ${}^-6 - 2 =$ _____

(d) ${}^-8 + 5 =$ _____

(e) ${}^-6 + 8 =$ _____

(f) $6 + {}^-8 =$ _____

(g) $8 + {}^-15 =$ _____

(h) $8 - 14 =$ _____

(i) ${}^-3 - 8 =$ _____

3 Complete the addition tables.

(a)

+	⁻3	⁻1	1	3	5
⁻5					
⁻3					
⁻1		⁻2			
1					6
3					

(b)

+	⁻7	⁻6	⁻2	1
⁻4				
⁻2				
⁻1			⁻3	
6				7

4 Write down the next four terms in each sequence.

(a) ${}^-9, {}^-7, {}^-5, {}^-3,$ _____, _____, _____, _____

(b) ${}^-2, {}^-6, {}^-10, {}^-14,$ _____, _____, _____, _____

(c) ${}^-21, {}^-16, {}^-11, {}^-6,$ _____, _____, _____, _____

6.2 Subtracting integers

1 **(a)** Complete these subtractions:

(i) $3 - 3 = 0$

$3 - 2 = 1$

$3 - 1 = $ _____

$3 - 0 = $ _____

$3 - {}^-1 = $ _____

$3 - {}^-2 = $ _____

(ii) $5 - 2 = $ _____

$5 - 1 = $ _____

$5 - 0 = $ _____

$5 - {}^-1 = $ _____

$5 - {}^-2 = $ _____

$5 - {}^-3 = $ _____

(iii) $11 - 4 = $ _____

$11 - 3 = $ _____

$11 - 2 = $ _____

$11 - 1 = $ _____

$11 - 0 = $ _____

$11 - {}^-1 = $ _____

I can do
this page!

(b) What pattern do you see?

_____

(c) Complete: Subtracting a negative number is the same as _____ a positive number.

2 Complete:

(a) $6 - {}^-3 = 6 + 3 = $ _____

(b) $5 - {}^-4 = $ _____

(c) $4 - {}^-4 = $ _____

(d) ${}^-3 - {}^-5 = $ _____

(e) ${}^-6 - {}^-4 = $ _____

(f) $12 - {}^-9 = $ _____

(g) $16 - {}^-11 = $ _____

(h) ${}^-13 - {}^-11 = $ _____

(i) ${}^-24 - {}^-17 = $ _____

(j) $17 - {}^-24 = $ _____

3 Complete the subtraction tables.

(a)

–	5	3	1	⁻1	⁻3
4	1				
2			⁻1		
0					
⁻2					
⁻4					

(b)

–	⁻7	⁻4	⁻1	2	5
⁻4					
⁻2					
⁻1					
0					
1					
2					3

4 The temperature in New York fell overnight from 3°C to ⁻5°C. By how much did the temperature fall?

_____

5* The Blue Mountain Peak in Jamaica is 7402 feet above sea level. The Dead Sea is 1312 feet below sea level. What is the difference in height between these two locations?

_____

6.3 Multiplying and dividing integers

1 Complete:

(a) $^-3 \times 4 = {}^-3 + {}^-3 + {}^-3 + {}^-3 =$

(b) $^-2 \times 6 = {}^-2 + {}^-2 + {}^-2 + {}^-2 + {}^-2 + {}^-2 =$

(c) $^-5 \times 3 =$

(d) $^-8 \times 4 =$

(e) $^-9 \times 5 =$

I can do
this page!

2 Work out:

(a) $^-3 \times 5 = \underline{\hspace{2cm}}$

(b) $^-4 \times 7 = \underline{\hspace{2cm}}$

(c) $^-3 \times 8 = \underline{\hspace{2cm}}$

(d) $^-8 \times 3 = \underline{\hspace{2cm}}$

(e) $^-6 \times 4 = \underline{\hspace{2cm}}$

(f) $4 \times {}^-6 = \underline{\hspace{2cm}}$

(g) $4 \times {}^-3 = \underline{\hspace{2cm}}$

(h) $7 \times {}^-3 = \underline{\hspace{2cm}}$

(i) $4 \times {}^-12 = \underline{\hspace{2cm}}$

3 (a) Complete the multiplications.

(i) $^-4 \times 3 = {}^-12$

$^-4 \times 2 = {}^-8$

$^-4 \times 1 = \underline{\hspace{1cm}}$

$^-4 \times 0 = \underline{\hspace{1cm}}$

$^-4 \times {}^-1 = \underline{\hspace{1cm}}$

$^-4 \times {}^-2 = \underline{\hspace{1cm}}$

(ii) $^-3 \times 2 = {}^-6$

$^-3 \times 1 = \underline{\hspace{1cm}}$

$^-3 \times 0 = \underline{\hspace{1cm}}$

$^-3 \times {}^-1 = \underline{\hspace{1cm}}$

$^-3 \times {}^-2 = \underline{\hspace{1cm}}$

$^-3 \times {}^-3 = \underline{\hspace{1cm}}$

(iii) $^-5 \times {}^-3 = \underline{\hspace{1cm}}$

$^-5 \times 2 = \underline{\hspace{1cm}}$

$^-5 \times 1 = \underline{\hspace{1cm}}$

$^-5 \times 0 = \underline{\hspace{1cm}}$

$^-5 \times {}^-1 = \underline{\hspace{1cm}}$

$^-5 \times {}^-2 = \underline{\hspace{1cm}}$

(b) What pattern do you see?

_____

_____

(c) Complete: Multiplying a negative number by a negative number gives an answer that is _____.

4 Work out:

(a) $3 \times 4 = \underline{\hspace{2cm}}$

(b) $^-3 \times 4 = \underline{\hspace{2cm}}$

(c) $^-3 \times {}^-4 = \underline{\hspace{2cm}}$

(d) $^-5 \times 6 = \underline{\hspace{2cm}}$

(e) $^-5 \times {}^-6 = \underline{\hspace{2cm}}$

(f) $^-6 \times {}^-5 = \underline{\hspace{2cm}}$

(g) $^-7 \times {}^-3 = \underline{\hspace{2cm}}$

(h) $7 \times {}^-3 = \underline{\hspace{2cm}}$

(i) $^-8 \times {}^-4 = \underline{\hspace{2cm}}$

5 Complete:

(a) $3 \times \underline{\hspace{1cm}} = {}^-6$

(b) $^-2 \times \underline{\hspace{1cm}} = {}^-8$

(c) $^-3 \times \underline{\hspace{1cm}} = 9$

(d) $\underline{\hspace{1cm}} \times 4 = {}^-24$

(e) $\underline{\hspace{1cm}} \times {}^-5 = {}^-20$

(f) $^-4 \times \underline{\hspace{1cm}} = 36$

(g) $\underline{\hspace{1cm}} \times {}^-6 = 24$

(h) $\underline{\hspace{1cm}} \times {}^-9 = {}^-72$

(i) $^-7 \times \underline{\hspace{1cm}} = 42$

I can do
this page!

6 Complete these multiplication tables:

(a)

×	-2	-1	0	2	4
3					12
1		-1			
-1					
-2					
-3					

(b)

×	4	1	-2	-5	-8
2	8		-4		
-1					
-4					
-7					
-10					

7 Complete:

(a) $^-2 \times 7 = ^-14$

so $^-14 \div 7 = $ _____

(b) $^-3 \times 6 = ^-18$

so $^-18 \div 6 = $ _____

(c) $4 \times ^-3 = ^-12$

so $^-12 \div ^-3 = $ _____

(d) $^-3 \times ^-4 = 12$

so $12 \div ^-4 = $ _____

(e) $^-5 \times ^-3 = 15$

so $15 \div ^-5 = $ _____

(f) $12 \times ^-4 = ^-48$

so $^-48 \div ^-4 = $ _____

8 Complete:

(i) A negative number divided by a positive number gives a _____ answer.

(ii) A negative number divided by a negative number gives a _____ answer.

9 Work out:

(a) $6 \div ^-3 = $ _____

(b) $^-9 \div 3 = $ _____

(c) $^-9 \div ^-3 = $ _____

(d) $^-12 \div 6 = $ _____

(e) $^-15 \div ^-5 = $ _____

(f) $^-18 \div 6 = $ _____

(g) $42 \div ^-7 = $ _____

(h) $^-18 \div ^-3 = $ _____

(i) $^-63 \div 9 = $ _____

10 Complete the division squares.

(a)

÷	6	4	2	-2	-4	-6
-2						
-1						
1		4				
2			1			-3

(b)

÷	12	6	-6	-12	-18
-3					
-2					
-1		-6			
2					
3	4				

Multiple choice 2

In each question, circle the correct answer.

1 E = {factors of 12}

F = {prime numbers up to 20}

What is E∩F?

A {2}   **B** {1, 2}   **C** {2, 3}   **D** {1, 2, 3}

2 X = {1, 2, 3, 4, 5, 6}

Y = {factors of 6}

What is X∪Y?

A X   **B** Y   **C** {2, 3, 6} **D** {1, 4, 5}

3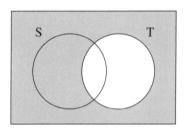

In the Venn diagram, the shaded portion is represented by:

A S∩T   **B** S∪T   **C** S′   **D** T′

4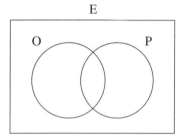

In the Venn diagram:

E = {whole numbers}

O = {odd numbers}

P = {prime numbers}

Which statement is true?

A 2 ∈ P

B 2 ∈ O

C 2 ∈ O∩P

D 2 ∈ (O ∪ P)′

Use the Venn diagram to answer Questions 5 and 6.

I can do this page!

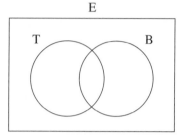

E = {boys}

T = {tall boys}

B = {boys who play basketball}

5 The set of short boys can be represented by:

A T′   **B** B′   **C** T∪B   **D** T∩B

6 What is T∩B′?

A Tall boys who play basketball

B Short boys who play basketball

C Tall boys who do not play basketball

D Short boys who do not play basketball

7 Alleyne walks 3200 m. How much is this in kilometres?

A 0.032 km   **B** 0.32 km

C 3.2 km   **D** 32 km

8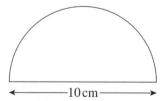

A semicircle has diameter 10 cm. What is its perimeter? (Take $\pi = 3.14$)

A 15.7 m   **B** 25.7 m   **C** 31.4 m   **D** 41.4 m

9

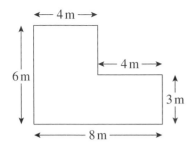

The diagram shows an L-shaped room. What is its area?

A 21 m²   **B** 24 m²   **C** 36 m²   **D** 48 m²

10

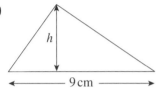

A triangle with base length 9 cm has area 36 cm². What is its vertical height?

A 2 cm   **B** 4 cm   **C** 6 cm   **D** 8 cm

11

A tin of milk has a circular base with diameter 10 cm. What is the area of the base? (Take π = 3.14)

A 31.4 cm²

B 62.8 cm²

C 78.5 cm²

D 314 cm²

12

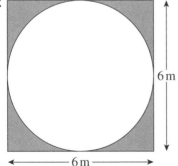

A square room of side 6 m has a tile pattern, as shown in the diagram. White tiles are in the form of a circle with diameter 6 m and blue tiles cover the remainder of the room. What area do the blue tiles cover? (Take π = 3.14)

A 1.68 m² **B** 7.74 m² **C** 16 m² **D** 77.04 m²

13 On a map, 2 cm represents 7 km. What is its scale?

A 1:3.5   **B** 1:3500   **C** 1:35 000   **D** 1:350 000

14 A map shows the distance between two towns as 5 cm. What is the actual distance if the scale of the map is 1:20 000?

A 4 km   **B** 1 km   **C** 0.4 km   **D** 0.1 km

15 The temperature in Iceland on five days is shown in the table.

Day 1	Day 2	Day 3	Day 4	Day 5
8°C	-3°C	-7°C	0°C	-4°C

Which day was the coldest?

A Day 1   **B** Day 3   **C** Day 4   **D** Day 5

16 What is 6 + ⁻8?

A ⁻2   **B** 2   **C** 14   **D** ⁻14

17 The temperature in New York on one day in January was ⁻7°C. The next day the temperature rose by 3°C. What was the new temperature?

A ⁻10°C   **B** ⁻4°C   **C** 4°C   **D** 10°C

18 What is the missing number in the pattern?

⁻12, ⁻7, ☐, 3, 8

A ⁻3   **B** ⁻2   **C** ⁻1   **D** 0

19 What is

⁻6 – ⁻4 – 3?

A 1   **B** ⁻5   **C** ⁻7   **D** ⁻13

20 What is the image of 1 under the map $y \rightarrow x - 3$?

A ⁻2   **B** ⁻4   **C** 2   **D** 4

Check your answers in the back of the book:

$$\text{Score} = \frac{\quad}{20}$$

Relations and graphs

7.1 Arrow diagrams and mappings

1 Complete these arrow diagrams:

(a) is 5 less than **(b)** is 3 times **(c)** is a factor of

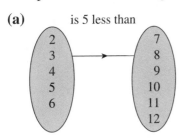 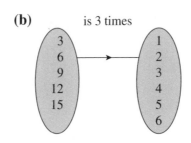 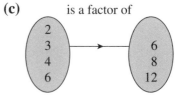

I can do this page!

2 X = {1, 2, 3, 4}, Y = {1, 2, 3, 4, 5, 6, 7, 8}

Draw arrow diagrams from set X to set Y for the rules given.

(a) Add 3 **(b)** Multiply by 2 **(c)** Multiply by 2, subtract 1

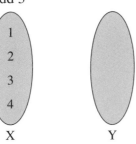 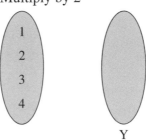 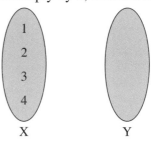

3 Describe the rule for these mappings:

(a) 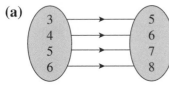 **(b)** 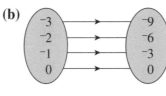 **(c)**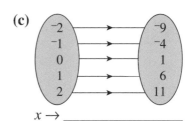

$x \rightarrow$ _____ $x \rightarrow$ _____ $x \rightarrow$ _____

4 Given X = {⁻2, ⁻1, 0, 1, 2} and Y = {⁻8, ⁻7, ⁻6, ⁻5, ⁻4 ⁻3, ⁻2, ⁻1, 0, 1, 2, 3, 4, 5, 6, 7, 8},
draw arrow graphs to show the mappings given.

(a) $x \rightarrow x + 3$ **(b)** $x \rightarrow 2x - 3$ **(c)** $x \rightarrow 3x + 2$

  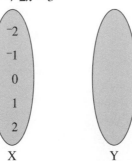 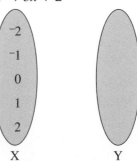

7.2 Plotting graphs

1 Plot the points on the axes given.

(a) ($^-$2, 1), ($^-$1, 2), (0, 3), (1, 4)

(b) ($^-$3, $^-$2), ($^-$2, $^-$1), ($^-$1, 0), (0, 1), (1, 2), (2, 3)

(c) ($^-$1, 7), (0, 6), (1, 5), (2, 4), (3, 3), (4, 2), (5, 1), (6, 0)

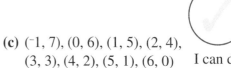

I can do this page!

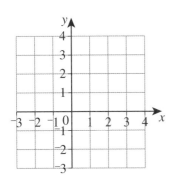
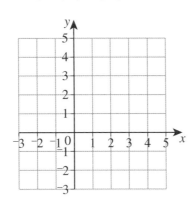

2 **(a)** Complete the input and output table for the number machine.

INPUT → [+5] → [×2] → OUTPUT

Input, x	$^-$2	$^-$1	0	1	2	3	4
Output, y				12			

(b) Plot the ordered pairs on the axes.

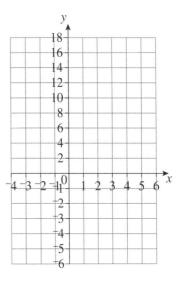

3* The graphs show the mapping of set X to set Y.
What is the rule for each map?

(a)

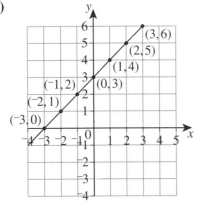

Rule: $y =$ _____

(b)

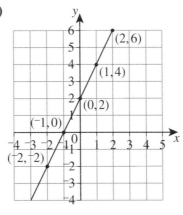

Rule: $y =$ _____

(c)

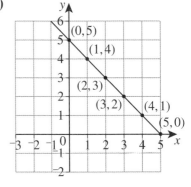

Rule: $y =$ _____

7.3 Reading graphs

1 The graph shows the rainfall in millimetres over a seven-day
    period in Maypen.

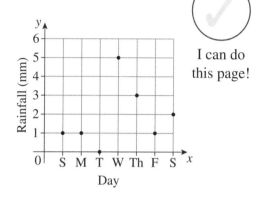

    (a) What was the rainfall on Friday? _____

    (b) On what day was there 2 mm of rain? _____

    (c) Which day was the wettest? _____

I can do
this page!

2 The graph shows the cost of baby ribbon by length.

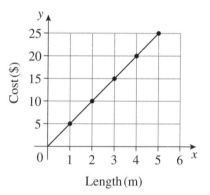

    (a) How much does 3 m of ribbon cost? _____

    (b) How much ribbon can I buy for $25? _____

    (c) What is the cost of 2.5 m of ribbon? _____

3 The graph shows the height in centimetres of a tomato
    plant at weekly intervals.

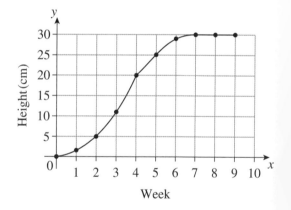

    (a) When was the plant 5 cm tall? _____

    (b) How tall was the plant in the 5th week? _____

    (c) When did the plant seem to stop growing? _____

    (d) When was the plant 23 cm tall? _____

4 Jason collected a number of worms and measured their lengths.
    He plotted his results on a graph.

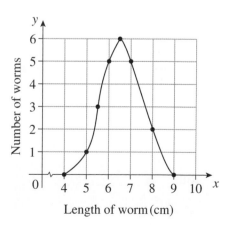

    (a) What was the length of the longest worm? _____

    (b) How many worms were 5.5 cm in length? _____

    (c) What length of worm was most common? _____

5 The table shows the height of Dexter at different ages.

Age	10	11	12	13	14	15
Height (cm)	125	130	140	150	155	160

(a) Plot these points on the graph and connect them.

(b) Use your graph to find Dexter's:

(i) age when he is 135 cm tall _____

(ii) height when he is $13\frac{1}{2}$ years _____

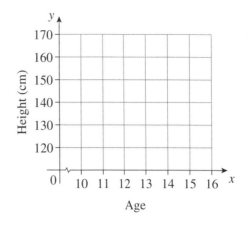

I can do this page!

6 The temperature at various times on a given day are shown in the table.

Time	6 am	9 am	12 noon	3 pm	6 pm	9 pm
Temperature (°C)	26	28	31	30	26	24

(a) Plot these points on the graph and connect them.

(b) What is the temperature at 10 am?

_____

(c) When is the temperature 27°C?

_____ and _____

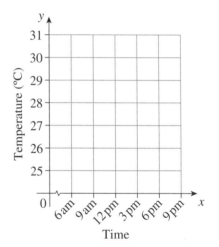

7* The area of a circle for different radii is given in the table.

Radius (cm)	1	2	3	4	5
Area (cm²)	8.14	12.56	28.26	50.24	78.5

(a) Plot these points on the graph and connect them.

(b) Use your graph to find:

(i) area of a circle with radius 3.5 cm

_____

(ii) radius of a circle with area 40 cm²

_____

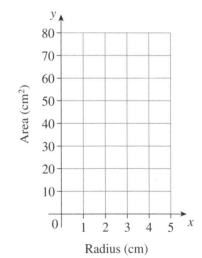

7.4 Graphs of relations

1 **(a)** Complete the arrow diagram for the map $x \rightarrow 3x + 2$.

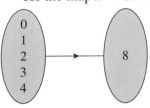

(b) Complete the same mapping in table form.

x	0	1	2	3	4
y			8		

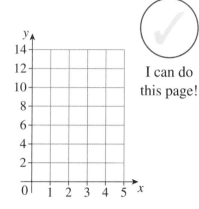

I can do this page!

(c) Write the mapping as a set of ordered pairs.

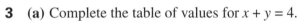

(d) Plot these ordered pairs on the axes.

2 **(a)** Complete the table of values for $y = x + 3$.

x	-3	-2	-1	0	1	2	3
y					4		

(b) Draw the graph of $y = x + 3$ on the axes.

(c) Use your graph to find the value of y when $x = 2\frac{1}{2}$.

$y = $ _____

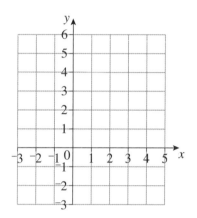

3 **(a)** Complete the table of values for $x + y = 4$.

x	-3	-2	-1	0	1	2	3	4	5
y							1		

(b) Draw the graph of $x + y = 4$ on the axes.

(c) What do you think the value of y is when $x = 6$?

$y = $ _____

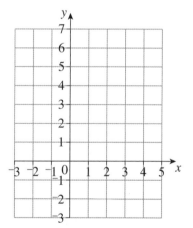

4 **(a)** Complete the table of values for $y = 3x - 4$.

x	-1	0	1	2	3
y			-1		

(b) Plot the points on the axes and join them with a straight line.

(c) For what value of x is y equal to 4?

$x = $ _____

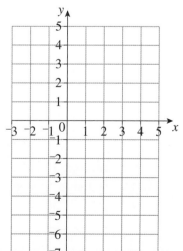

5 **(a)** Complete the table of values for $y = 6 - x$.

x	-3	-2	-1	0	1	2	3	4	5	6
y			7					2		

(b) Draw the graph of $y = 6 - x$ on the axes.

(c) Use your graph to find the value of x when $y = 2\frac{1}{2}$.

$x =$ _____

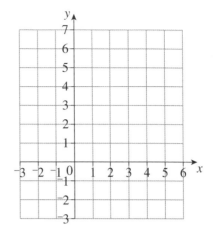

I can do
this page!

6 **(a)** Complete the table of values for $y = 12 - 4x$.

x	-3	-2	-1	0	1	2	3	4
y	24			12				-4

(b) Draw the graph of $y = 12 - 4x$ on the axes.

(c) For what value of x is $y = 22$?

$x =$ _____

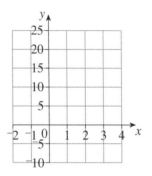

7 **(a)** Complete the table of values for the equations $y = 2x - 1$

x	-2	-1	0	1	2	3	4	5
y				1			7	

and $y = x + 3$.

x	-2	-1	0	1	2	3	4	5
y				4				

(b) Draw the graphs of the equations on the axes.

(c) At what point do the two lines intersect? _____

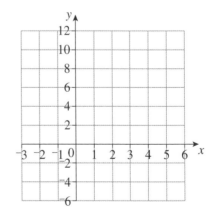

7.5 Gradients and intercepts

1 Find the gradient and intercept of the lines shown.

(a)

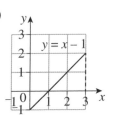

Gradient = _____

Intercept, y = _____

(b)

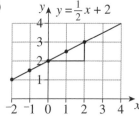

Gradient = _____

Intercept, y = _____

I can do
this page!

> **Remember**
>
> Gradient $= \dfrac{\text{vertical rise}}{\text{horizontal shift}}$

2 Write down the gradient and intercept of these lines.

(a) $y = 2x - 3$

Gradient =

Intercept =

(b) $y = 4x + 2$

Gradient =

Intercept =

(c) $y = 5x - 9$

Gradient =

Intercept =

> **Remember**
>
> The line $y = mx + c$
> has gradient $= m$
> intercept $= c$

3 On the axes draw lines with:

(a) Gradient 3 through the point (1, 1)

(b) Gradient 2, intercept ⁻2

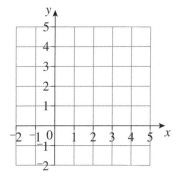

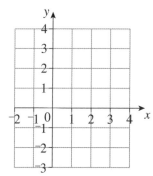

4

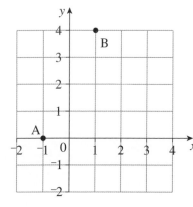

In the graph,

(a) what are the coordinates of A and B

A _____ , B _____.

(b) what is the gradient of the line segment joining A to B

(c) what is the equation of the line passing through A and B?

7.6 Inequalities

1 The number line shows the inequality $x < 3$

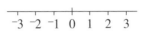

 I can do this page!

Show these inequalities on the number lines below.

(a) $x > 2$ **(b)** $x \geq {}^-1$ **(c)** $x < {}^-2$

2 **(a)** On the graphs draw the following lines:

     (i) $x = 2$ **(ii)** $y = 3$ **(iii)** $x = -1$ **(iv)** $y = -2$

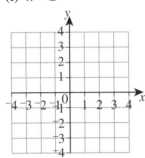 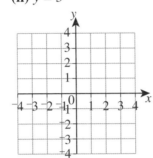 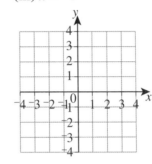 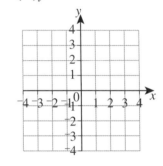

   (b) Now shade the regions given below.

     (i) $x > 2$ **(ii)** $y < 3$ **(iii)** $x \leq -1$ **(iv)** $y \geq -2$

3 Write the inequality represented by the shaded regions in these graphs:

   (a)   **(b)**   **(c)**   **(d)**

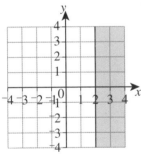 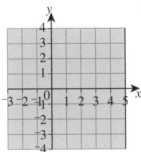 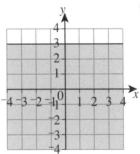 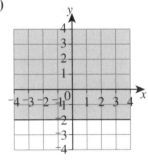

4 On the axes, show the regions given by:

     (a) $0 \leq x \leq 1$ **(b)** $x > 2, y > 1$ **(c)** $x \geq {}^-1, y < 2$ **(d)** $y < x$

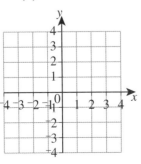 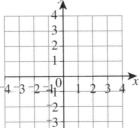 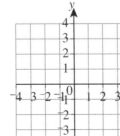 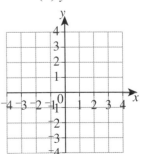

8.1 Reflections

1 Complete these diagrams to reflect shapes in the mirror line:

(a)

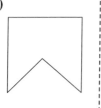

(b)

B

✓

I can do
this page!

2 Draw the images of the triangles after reflection in the:

(a) *x*-axis

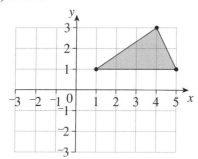

(b) *y*-axis

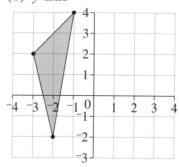

3 Triangle PQR is reflected in the *x*-axis.

(a) Draw its image P′Q′R′ on the graph.

(b) Write down the coordinates of P′Q′R′:

    P′(,   ), Q′(,   ), R′(,   )

(c) Draw the image P″Q″R″ after reflection of triangle P′Q′R′ in the *y*-axis.

(d) Write down the coordinates of P″Q″R″:

    P″(,   ), Q″(,   ), R″(,   )

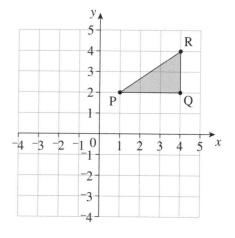

4 (a) On the axes draw the triangle ABC, with A(-2, 1), B(-1, -3), C(0, 0).

(b) Draw the line *x* = 1.

(c) Draw the image A′B′C′ of triangle ABC after reflection in the line *x* = 1.

(d) What are the coordinates of A′B′C′?

    A′(,   ), B′(,   ), C′(,   )

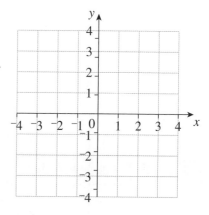

8.2 Translations

1 Describe the translations shown. The first one has been done for you.

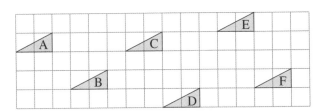

Remember

A **translation** is a sliding movement in a particular direction.

I can do this page!

(a) A → B   3 right, 2 down

(b) A → C   _____

(c) B → E   _____

(d) F → E   _____

(e) C → B   _____

(f) D → A   _____

2 Show the image of these triangles after the given translations.

(a) 2 right, 1 up

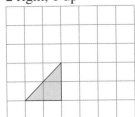

(b) 1 left, 2 down

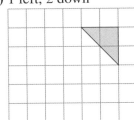

(c) 3 left, 2 up

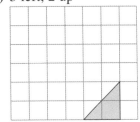

(d) 2 right, 2 down

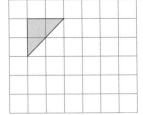

3 The triangle ABC, with A($^-$2, 1), B(0, 4), C(1, 1) is translated 2 units right, 3 units down.

(a) Show the image A′B′C′ of triangle ABC on the graph.

(b) Write down the coordinates of A′B′C′.

   A′(,   ), B′(,   ), C′(,   )

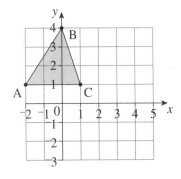

4* The rectangle A($^-$3, 0), B($^-$3, 1), C($^-$1, 1), D($^-$1, 0) is translated 3 units right, 3 units up.

(a) Show rectangle ABCD on the graph.

(b) Show its image $A_1B_1C_1D_1$ after translation.

(c) Rectangle $A_1B_1C_1D_1$ is translated 1 unit left, 1 unit down. Show its image $A_2B_2C_2D_2$ on the graph.

(d) What single translation will send ABCD→ $A_2B_2C_2D_2$? _____

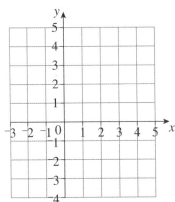

8.3 Vectors and translations

1 Write column vectors to describe these translations.

(a)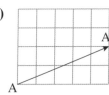

(b)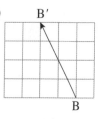

(c)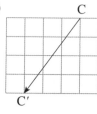

$$\overrightarrow{AA'} = \begin{pmatrix} \\ \end{pmatrix}$$

$$\overrightarrow{BB'} = \begin{pmatrix} \\ \end{pmatrix}$$

$$\overrightarrow{CC'} = \begin{pmatrix} \\ \end{pmatrix}$$

I can do
this page!

2 On the grids, draw translations represented by the column vectors.

(a) $\overrightarrow{AA'} = \begin{pmatrix} 2 \\ 1 \end{pmatrix}$

(b) $\overrightarrow{BB'} = \begin{pmatrix} -2 \\ 1 \end{pmatrix}$

(c) $\overrightarrow{CC'} = \begin{pmatrix} 1 \\ -2 \end{pmatrix}$

(d) $\overrightarrow{DD'} = \begin{pmatrix} -1 \\ -2 \end{pmatrix}$

(e) $\overrightarrow{EE'} = \begin{pmatrix} 0 \\ -2 \end{pmatrix}$

(f) $\overrightarrow{FF'} = \begin{pmatrix} -2 \\ 0 \end{pmatrix}$

3 Write a column vector to describe the translation of shape X to its image shape B.

(a)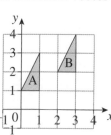

(b)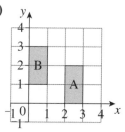

(c)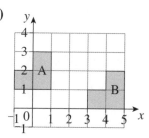

_____

_____

_____

4 Draw the image A'B'C' of triangle ABC after translation represented by:

(a) $\begin{pmatrix} 1 \\ 1 \end{pmatrix}$

(b) $\begin{pmatrix} -2 \\ 1 \end{pmatrix}$

(c) $\begin{pmatrix} 1 \\ -2 \end{pmatrix}$

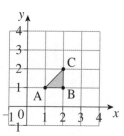

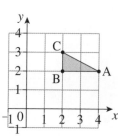

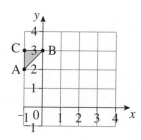

8.4 Rotations

1 Draw the images of these shapes after a rotation through 180° about the point O.

(a)

(b)

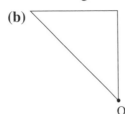

I can do
this page!

2 What is the order of rotational symmetry of these shapes?

(a)    **(b)** 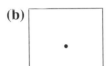   **(c)**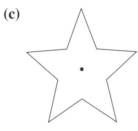

> **Remember**
>
> The number of times a shape
> fits onto itself after a complete
> turn is the **order of rotational
> symmetry.**

_____   _____   _____

(d) 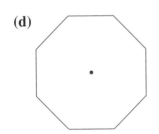   **(e)** 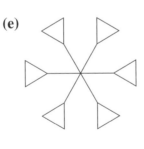   **(f)**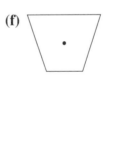

_____   _____   _____

(g) 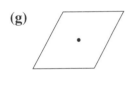   **(h)**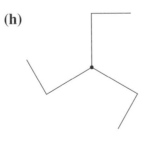

_____   _____

3 Draw two shapes with rotational symmetry of order:

   (a) 4   **(b)** 5

Statistics

9.1 Frequency tables and charts

1 The shoe sizes of 30 children are:

5, 6, 5, 7, 8, 4, 7, 7, 8, 5

6, 6, 5, 4, 7, 9, 4, 7, 5, 6

5, 7, 8, 7, 7, 6, 5, 5, 6, 7

Shoe size	Tally	Frequency
4		
5		
6		
7		
8		
9		

I can do this page!

(a) Complete the frequency table to show this data.

(b) Which is the most common size? _____

2 The bar chart shows the reading levels of a group of students.

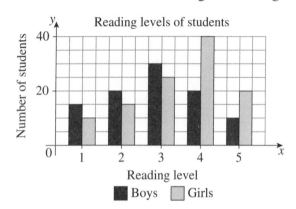

(a) How many boys are reading at Level 1?   _____

(b) How many students are reading at Level 3?   _____

(c) How many more girls than boys are reading at Level 4?   _____

(d) Are girls reading better than boys in this group of students? Explain.

_____

3 The chart shows the distribution of the masses of some packages.

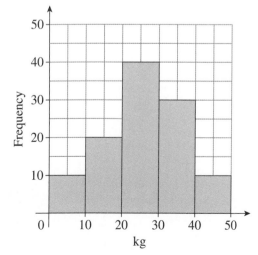

(a) How many packages had a mass of under 10 kg? _____

(b) How many packages had a mass of 30 kg or more? _____

(c) How many packages are there altogether? _____

4 The scores obtained by 40 students in an exam were:

24, 58, 64, 75, 42, 65, 72, 81, 91, 76
47, 62, 68, 58, 55, 57, 61, 63, 70, 68
42, 38, 49, 57, 58, 64, 62, 80, 81, 49
60, 64, 52, 78, 68, 57, 63, 65, 67, 51

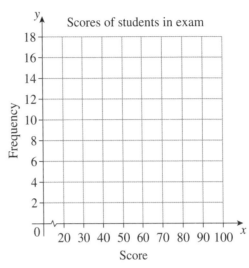

(a) Complete the frequency table for this data.

Score	Tally	Frequency
20–29		
30–39		
40–49		
50–59		
60–69		
70–79		
80–89		
90–99		

(b) Complete the chart to show this data.

(c) How many students scored over 60%? _____

5* The times taken for 30 mice to run though a maze, in seconds, is shown below.

31	42	58	37	44	56	51	34	43	47
38	46	46	52	33	58	34	31	45	49
42	55	54	38	41	44	48	38	41	32

(a) Complete the frequency table for this data.

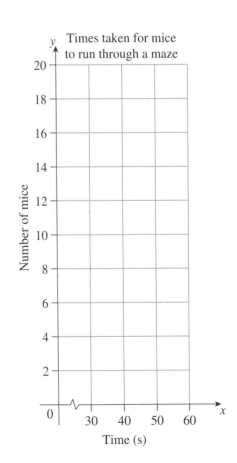

Time to go through maze (s)	Tally	Number of mice
31–35		
36–40		
41–45		
46–50		
51–55		
56–60		

(b) Complete the chart to show this data.

(c) What is the most frequent time recorded by mice through the maze?

_____

9.2 Pie charts

1 The grades of 36 students on a science test are shown below.

Grade	Number of students
A	7
B	15
C	10
D	4

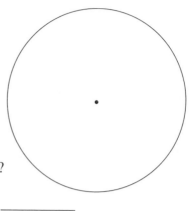

I can do
this page!

(a) What size of angle would represent one student on a pie chart?

_____

(b) What size angle would represent the A-graded students?

_____

(c) Complete the pie chart above to show the information.

2 In a survey 120 people were interviewed about their movie preferences. The results were:

Movie type	Number of people
Action	50
Comedy	15
Drama	12
Romance	35
Sci-fi	8

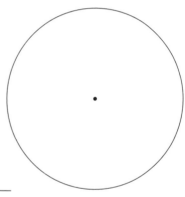

(a) What size of angle would represent one person on a pie chart? _____

(b) Complete the pie chart to show this data.

3 Customer preference for cakes is shown in the table.

Cake type	Number of people	Size of angle in pie chart
Coconut	40	
Fruit	60	
Chocolate	80	
Orange	60	

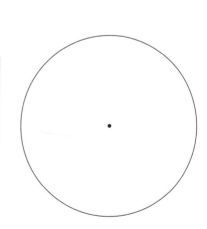

(a) How many customers were there? _____

(b) Complete the table.

(c) Complete the pie chart to show this data.

4 Of 80 motorists charged by the police, the offences were:

Offence	Number of motorists	Size of angle on pie chart
No insurance	5	
No licence	20	
Broken lights	35	
Bald tyres	12	
Other	3	

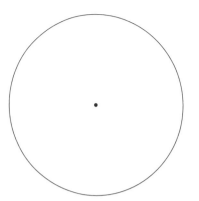

I can do
this page!

(a) Complete the table.

(b) Complete the pie chart to show this data.

5 The pie chart shows the bounds of soap powder sold in a store on one day.

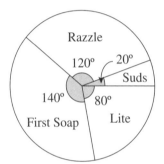

(a) If 90 packets of soap powder were sold, what size of angle represents one packet of soap powder?

_____

(b) How many packets of Razzle were sold?

_____

(c) How many packets of Suds were sold?

_____

6 The pie chart shows the share of the vote gained by each of three parties in an election.

If 10 000 people voted, find the number of people voting for:

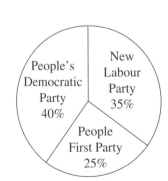

(a) the People's Democratic Party

_____

(b) the People First Party

_____

9.3 Line graphs

1   The graphs shows the average monthly temperature in degrees Fahrenheit in Smalltown.

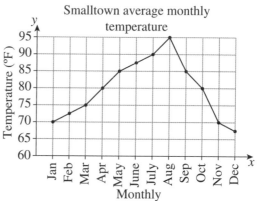

Smalltown average monthly temperature

I can do this page!

   (a) What was the average temperature in March?

   _____

   (b) In what month was the average temperature 90°F?

   _____

   (c) In which months did the temperature reach 80°F?

   _____

   (d) What was the lowest average monthly temperature?

   _____

   (e) Why do you think the temperature axis started at 60°F and not 0°F?

   _____

2   Look at the graphs showing left expectancy of men in Jamaica over the last 60 years.

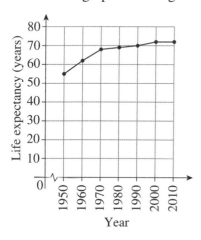   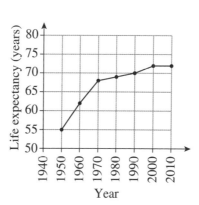

   (a) Why do the graphs look different?

   _____

   (b) Would you say there has been a dramatic increase in life expectancy over the last 60 years?

   _____

   (c) Which graph gives a better reflection of changes in life expectancy? Why?

   _____

(d) The table shows life expectation for women in the same period.

Year	1950	1960	1970	1980	1990	2000	2010
Life expectancy	59	67	70	72	73	76	75

Plot these values on both graphs.

(e) Have there been greater increases in life expectancy for women than for men in the last 60 years?

_____

3* The table below shows the number of live births per 1000 people in Jamaica since 1960.

Year	1960	1970	1980	1990	2000	2010
Number of live births	41	36	29	25	21	16

(a) Choose a suitable scale and plot these points on a graph.

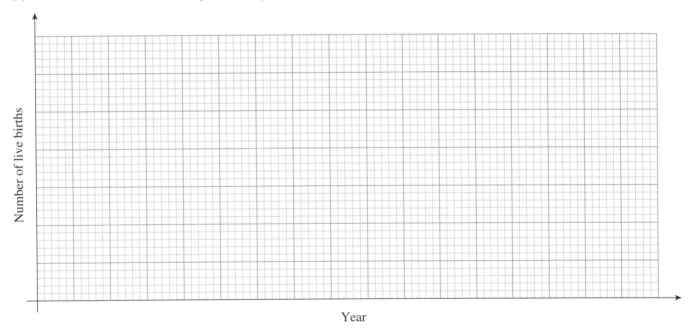

(b) Does it make sense to join these points with a line? Why?

_____

(c) Should you use a straight line or a curved line to join the points? Why?

_____

(d) What would you predict as the number of live births per 1000 people in 2020?

_____

I can do
this page!

9.4 Averages

I can do
this page!

> **Remember**
>
> A set of data can be described by the three types of **average**:
>
> **mode** = the most common item in any set of data
>
> **median** = the middle number when the data is arranged in size order
>
> **mean** = $\dfrac{\text{sum of the data values}}{\text{number of data values}}$
>
> For example: The number of hours spent doing homework in a
>   week by a group of children is
>
>   5   0   2   5   3   4   9
>
> The numbers arranged in size order are
>
>   0   2   3   4   5   5   9
>
> Mode = 5 hours   Median = 4 hours (middle number)
>
> Mean = $\dfrac{5+0+2+5+3+4+9}{7} = \dfrac{28}{7} = 4$ hours

1 Find the median of these numbers:

(a) 3, 7, 2, 5, 8

(b) 4, 2, 9, 11, 17, 6, 5, 8

(c) 91, 80, 103, 97, 92, 92, 87

2 The temperatures in °C at 12 noon in a particular week were

25, 25, 24, 28, 24, 25, 27

(a) What was the mean temperature?   _____

(b) Find the median temperature?   _____

(c) What is the mode?   _____

3 The shoe sizes of 11 people were

       8, 7, 8, 5, 4, 3, 9, 8, 10, 12, 6

(a) What is the mode?   _____

(b) Write the numbers in size order.
    What is the median size?   _____

(c) What is the mean size?

           Mean =

(d) In ordering more shoes, which average would a shoe store manager
    pay more attention to? Why?

    _____

    _____

4 Ten mice were weighed, and their masses in grams were:

34   28   36   27   30   30   34   38   31   30

(a) What was the modal mass?   _____

(b) What was the median mass?   _____

(c) What was the mean mass?

Mean =   _____

(d) Which average is a scientist more likely to use
when reporting the average mass of a mouse? Why?

_____

_____

I can do
this page!

5* The table shows the number of absences from school of a group of children.

Number of days absent	Frequency
0	8
1	6
2	5
3	5
4	0
5	1

(a) How many children were there in the group? _____

(b) What was the mode? _____

(c) Determine the median number of days absent _____

(d) Find the mean number of days a child from this group was
absent _____

6* (a) Throw a dice 30 times. Record your results in the frequency table.

Number	Tally	Frequency
1		
2		
3		
4		
5		
6		

(b) Find the:

(i) mode   _____

(ii) median   _____

(iii) mean   _____

Multiple choice 3

In each question, circle the correct answer.

1 Which of these arrow diagrams shows a function?

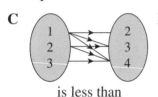

square root   is a factor of

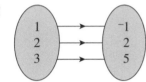

is less than   add seven

2

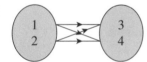

What rule does the mapping shown in the arrow diagram show?

A $x \rightarrow x - 2$ **B** $x \rightarrow x + 2$

C $x \rightarrow 4x - 5$ **D** $x \rightarrow 3x - 4$

3

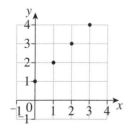

What ordered pairs are shown in the arrow diagram?

A (1, 3), (2, 4)

B (1, 4), (1, 3)

C (1, 3), (1, 4), (2, 3), (2, 4)

D (3, 1), (4, 1), (3, 2), (4, 2)

4

What is the rule for the mapping shown in the graph?

A $x \rightarrow x - 1$ **B** $x \rightarrow x + 1$

C $x \rightarrow 2x$ **D** $x \rightarrow 2x - 1$

I can do this page!

Use the graph to answer Questions 5 and 6.

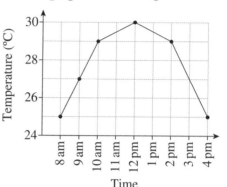

The graphs shows the temperature in Mandeville on a day in March.

5 What was the temperature at 11 am?
A 28.5°C **B** 29°C **C** 29.5°C **D** 30°C

6 When was the temperature 27°C?
A 9 am and 3 pm   **B** 9 am and 4 pm
C 8 am and 3 pm   **D** 8 am and 4 pm

7 Which graph shows the equation $y = 2x - 1$?

A 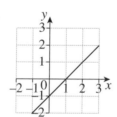   **B**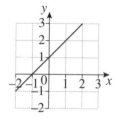

C 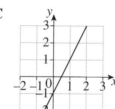   **D**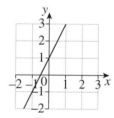

8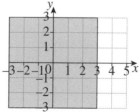

Which inequality represents the shaded region?

A $x < 3$ **B** $x > 3$
C $y < 3$ **D** $y > 3$

9

The point (⁻3, 2) is reflected in the y-axis. What is its image?

A (⁻3, ⁻2)   **B** (3, 2)
C (2, 3)   **D** (⁻2, ⁻3)

10 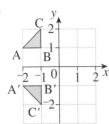 Describe the transformation that takes triangle ABC to triangle A′B′C′

A Reflection in the *x*-axis

B Reflection in the *y*-axis

C Reflection in the line $x = {}^-1$

D Reflection in the line $y = 1$

11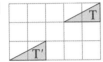

Which vector represents the translation that sends triangle T to triangle T′?

A $\begin{array}{c} 3 \\ 2 \end{array}$ **B** $\begin{array}{c} ^-3 \\ ^-2 \end{array}$ **C** $\begin{array}{c} ^-2 \\ 3 \end{array}$ **D** $\begin{array}{c} 2 \\ ^-3 \end{array}$

12 The point $(^-2, {}^-3)$ is translated by the vector $\begin{array}{c} 2 \\ 3 \end{array}$. What are the coordinates of its image?

A $(0, 0)$ **B** $(^-4, {}^-6)$ **C** $(^-4, 0)$ **D** $(0, {}^-6)$

13 The triangle ABC is rotated about B though 90° in a clockwise direction. Which diagram represents its image?

A   **B**

C   **D**

14 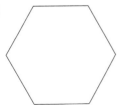 What is the order of symmetry of this regular hexagon?

A 0   **B** 4   **C** 6   **D** 8

Use the pie chart to answer Questions 15 and 16.

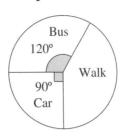

The pie chart shows how 60 students travel to Stratford School.

15 What fraction of students travel by car?

A $\dfrac{1}{2}$ **B** $\dfrac{1}{3}$ **C** $\dfrac{1}{4}$ **D** $\dfrac{1}{6}$

16 How many students walk?

A 20   **B** 25   **C** 30   **D** 35

Use the bar chart to answer Questions 17 and 18.

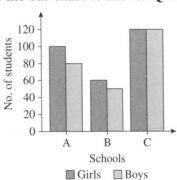

The chart shows the number of students entered for a mathematics exam at three different schools.

17 How many students were entered for mathematics at school A?

A 20   **B** 80   **C** 100   **D** 180

18 How many more girls were entered for mathematics at school C than at school B?

A 60   **B** 70   **C** 170   **D** 180

19 The number of goats kept by five farmers were:

12   3   14   13   6

What was the median number of goats kept?

A 5   **B** 6   **C** 10   **D** 12

20 A boy threw a dice five times with the following results.

Score	1	2	3	4	5	6
Number of times	0	0	2	1	2	0

What was the mean score?

A 2   **B** 3   **C** 4   **D** 5

Check your answers in the back of the book:

Score = $\dfrac{}{20}$

Patterns and algebra (10)

10.1 Numbers and patterns 1

1 (a) Circle the prime numbers in these number squares.

✓

I can do
this page!

(i)

1	2	3	4	5	6	7
8	9	10	11	12	13	14
15	16	17	18	19	20	21
22	23	24	25	26	27	28
29	30	31	32	33	34	35
36	37	38	39	40	41	42
43	44	45	46	47	48	49

(ii)

83	84	85	86	87	88	89	90
91	92	93	94	95	96	97	98
99	100	101	102	103	104	105	106
107	108	109	110	111	112	113	114
115	116	117	118	119	120	121	122
123	124	125	126	127	128	129	130
131	132	133	134	135	136	137	138
139	140	140	141	142	143	144	145

(b) Do you notice any patterns in the squares?

> ### Remember
> A **prime number** is a number with only two factors, 1 and itself.

2 (a) Circle the multiples of 3 in these number squares.

(i)

17	18	19	20	21	22
23	24	25	26	27	28
29	30	31	32	33	34
35	36	37	38	39	40
41	42	43	44	45	46
47	48	49	50	51	52

(ii)

107	108	109	110
111	112	113	114
115	116	117	118
119	120	121	122

(iii)

47	48	49	50	51
52	53	54	55	56
57	58	59	60	61
62	63	64	65	66
67	68	69	70	71

(b) What do you notice?

3

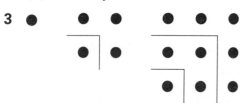

(a) Draw the next two shapes in this pattern below.

(b) Complete the table.

(c) What is the sum of the first 20 odd numbers?

Shape	Number of dots	Total
1	1	1
2	1 + 3	4
3	1 + 3 + 5	9
4		
5		
⋮		
10		

10.2 Numbers and patterns 2

1 Look at the pattern.

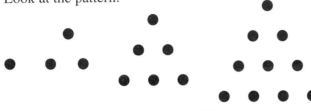

I can do
this page!

(a) Draw the next two shapes in this pattern.

(b) Complete the table.

Shape	Number of dots	Total
1	1	1
2	1 + 2	3
3	1 + 2 + 3	6
4	1 + 2 + 3 + 4	10
5		
6		
⋮		
10		

These numbers are called **triangle** numbers. Can you think why?

(c) How many dots will there be in the 15th shape? _____

2 Complete this table of triangle numbers:

Triangle no. position	6th	7th	8th	9th	10th	11th	12th	13th	14th	15th	16th	17th	18th	19th	20th
Triangle number						66					136				

(a) Complete these multiplication squares:

(i)

×	1	2	3	4	5	6	7	8	9
1	1	2	3	4	5	6	7		
2	2	4	6	8	10	12	14		
3	3	6	9	12	15	18	21		
4	4	8	12	16	20	24	28		
5	5	10	15	20	25	30	35		
6	6	12	18	24	30	36	42		
7	7	14	21	28	35	42	49		
8									
9									

(ii)

×	11	12	13	14	15	
11						
12			168			
13						
14		182				
15	175					

(b) In each square, circle the triangle numbers.

(c) What pattern can you see?

_____

(d) Do you think the pattern will continue for other multiplication squares? Why?

_____

10.3 Formulae

I can do
this page!

1 The formula for the nth triangle number is $T_n = \frac{1}{2} n(n + 1)$. What is

    (a) the 8th triangle number _____

    (b) the 14th triangle number _____

    (c) the 100th triangle number? _____

2 The formula that converts distance in yards, y, to feet, f, is $f = 3y$.

    What is

    (a) 6 yards in feet _____   **(b)** 54 feet in yards? _____

3 Temperatures measured in degrees Fahrenheit, F, are related to those measured in degrees Celsius, C, by the formula $F = 1.8C + 32$. Find the temperature in Fahrenheit when it is:

    (a) 35°C $F =$

    (b) 84°C $F =$

4 The area of a circle, A, is given by $A = \frac{\pi d^2}{4}$, where d is the diameter of the circle and $\pi = 3.14$. Find the area of circles with diameter

    (a) 8 cm $A =$

    (b) 13.2 cm $A =$

5 Write down a formula for the perimeter, p, of these shapes:

(a)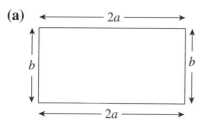

(b)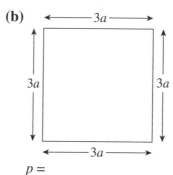

(c)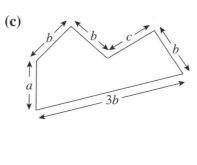

$p =$ $p =$ $p =$

6 Yams are sold for $\$ y$ per pound and potatoes for $\$ p$ per pound. What is the total cost, C of

    (a) 7 pounds of yams and 2 pounds of potatoes $C =$ _____

    (b) t pounds of yams and 4 pounds of potatoes? $C =$ _____

7* Brianna walks for 2 hours at a km/h and then runs for half an hour at b km/hr.

    (a) What is the total distance, d, that she travels? $d =$ _____

    (b) What is her average speed, v? $v =$ _____

10.4 Basic algebra

1 Simplify the following. The first one has been done for you.

(a) $3x + 4x - 6x = 7x - 6x = x$ _____

(b) $2y + y + 6y =$ _____

(c) $8x - 3x - 2y =$ _____

(d) $4x + 3y - x + y =$ _____

(e) $3x - 2y + 8x + 4y =$ _____

(f) $7x - 4y - 3x - 2y =$ _____

(g) $2x - y - 3z + 2y - x =$ _____

(h) $4x - 3y - 2z + 2y - 4z - x =$ _____

(i) $2x + 3 - 4y - 2 - 2y =$ _____

(j) $4 - 3x + 2y - 3 + 7z - 4y + 2x =$ _____

I can do this page!

2 Complete:

(a) $a^2 \times a^4 = a \times a \ \times \ a \times a \times a \times a =$

(b) $a^3 \times a^2 = a \times a \times a \times$_____ $= a^5$

(c) $a^4 \times a^3 =$

(d) $a^5 \times a^2 = a \times a \times a \times a \times a \times$

(e) $a^3 \times a^5 =$

> ### Remember
> $a \times a \times a \times a = a^4$
>
> $a \times a \times a \times a \times a = a^5$ etc.

How are the powers related in these products? _____

Complete: $a^m \times a^n = a^{\boxed{}}$

3 Complete:

(a) $a^5 \div a^2 = \dfrac{a \times a \times a \times a \times a}{a \times a} = a \times a \times a =$

(b) $a^6 \div a^4 = \dfrac{a \times a \times a \times a \times a \times a}{a \times a \times a \times a} =$

(c) $a^7 \div a^3 =$ $= a^4$

(d) $a^4 \div a =$ $=$

(e) $a^5 \div a^4 =$ $=$

How are the powers related in these divisions? _____

Complete $a^m \div a^n = a^{\boxed{}}$

4 Simplify:

(a) $a^6 \times a^7 =$ _____

(b) $b^8 \times b^4 =$ _____

(c) $a^7 \times a^8 =$ _____

(d) $b^2 \times b^3 \times b^4 =$ _____

(e) $a^6 \div a^2 =$ _____

(f) $b^9 \div b^3 =$ _____

5 Simplify:

(a) $3a^4 \times 2a^3$

(b) $\dfrac{7b^2 \times 2c^3}{4bc^2}$

(c) $\dfrac{(2a)^2 \times 3b^3}{5c^2ba}$

10.5 Brackets

1   Use the distributive law to find:

    (a) $13 \times 27 = 13 \times (20 + 7)$

           $= 13 \times 20 + 13 \times 7$

           $=$

           $=$ _____

    (b) $28 \times 32 = 28 \times (\quad + \quad)$

           $=$ _____

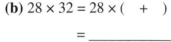

I can do
this page!

2   Expand the brackets. The first one has been done for you.

    (a) $4(3x - 4) = 4 \times 3x - 4 \times 4 = 12x - 16$

    (b) $3(x + 5) =$ **(c)** $6(2 - 3x) =$

    (d) $3(4x - 2y) =$ **(e)** $4x(x - y) =$

    (f) $3x^2(2x - y) =$ **(g)** $xy(4 - y^2) =$

3   Factorise. The first one has been done for you.

    (a) $4x - 8y = 4(x - 2y)$

    (b) $3x + 6y =$ **(c)** $7x + 21 =$

    (d) $6 - 18y =$ **(e)** $3x + 6 + 9y =$

    (f) $y^2 - y =$ **(g)** $3x^2y + xy - 4xy^2 =$

4   Simplify:

    (a) $3(x + y) + 2(x + y) =$

    (b) $4(2x - y) + 3(x - y) =$

    (c) $5(x - 2y) + 4(x - 3y) =$

    (d) $4(x - 3) + 5 + 2(x + 4) =$

    (e) $3x^2(4 - y) + 2(6x^2 - 3y) =$

    (f) $7xy(x - y) + 3xy(y - 2x) =$

5*   Use the diagrams to help you simplify:

    (a) $(x + 3)(x + 2) =$ _____   **(b)** $(x + 4)(x + 1) =$ _____

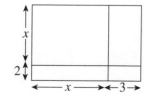
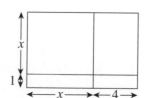

10.6 Linear equations

1 Use a flow diagram to solve these equations. The first one has been done for you.

I can do
this page!

(a) $x + 4 = 9$

$x = 5$

(b) $x - 5 = 8$

$x =$ _____

(c) $3x = 12$

$x =$ _____

(d) $\dfrac{x}{4} = 8$

$x =$ _____

(e) $2x - 1 = 7$

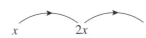

$x =$ _____

(f) $3x + 4 = 22$

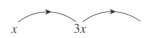

$x =$ _____

(g) $\dfrac{x}{2} + 5 = 7$

(h) $3(x - 2) = 15$

(i) $\dfrac{2x - 3}{4} = 5$

2 Use the balance idea to solve these equations:

(a) $x + 4 = 6$

$(-4)\ x =$

(b) $x - 5 = 4$

$(+5)\ x =$

(c) $4x = 20$

$(\div 4)\ x =$

(d) $2x + 3 = 7$

$(-3)\ 2x =$ ___

$(\div 2)\ x =$ _____

(e) $2x - 5 = 9$

$(+5)\ 2x =$

$(\div 2)\ x =$

(f) $3x - 7 = 14$

$(+7)\ 3x =$

$(\div 3)\ x =$

(g) $4x - 11 = 5$

$(+11)\ 4x =$

$(\div 4)\ x =$

(h) $3x + 4 = 2x + 7$

$(-2x)\ x + 4 =$

$(-4)\ x =$

(i) $5x - 3 = 4x + 5$

$(-4x)\ x - 3 =$

$(+3)\ x =$

3 Solve these equations:

(a) $4x - 3 = 5$

(b) $3x - 2 = 2x$

(c) $6 - x = 5x$

I can do
this page!

(d) $3x - 5 = 2x + 3$

(e) $6x + 2 = 2x + 10$

(f) $7x - 3 = 4x - 1$

(g) $4 - 3x = 2 + 2x$

(h) $3(x + 3) = 2x + 10$

(i) $6(2x - 1) = 4(x + 4)$

4 Remove the brackets, then simplify to solve these equations:

(a) $5x + 3(x + 2) = 22$

(b) $3(x - 2) + 2(x - 4) = 1$

(c) $2x + 3(2x - 4) = 7x + 2$

(d) $3(4x - 3) + 2(4 - x) = 9$

(e) $4(2x - 7) + 3(3x - 1) = 3(2 - x)$

(f) $3(4 - 2x) + 4(2 - 3x) = 5(1 - x)$

(h) $\dfrac{x - 4}{3} + 4 = 10$

(i) $\dfrac{2x - 3}{5} - 2 = 9$

10.7 Solving word problems

In each of these questions, first write down an equation, then solve it.

I can do
this page!

1 The result when adding 9 to a number is 28. What is the number?

_____

2 The sum of two consecutive numbers is 111. What are the numbers?

_____

3 A rectangle has length 8 cm longer than its width, w.

Find the width of the rectangle if it has perimeter 64 cm.

_____

4 Celine has $25 more than Adelle. How much does Adelle have if together they have $175?

_____

5 A school has 40 fewer boys than girls. How many girls are in the school if the school's population is 420?

_____

6* Amos is x years old. In ten years time he will be three times his current age. What is his current age?

_____

10.8 Change the subject of a formula

1   Use a function machine to make x the subject of these formulae.

I can do
this page!

(a) $y = 2x + c$

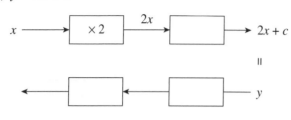

$x = \underline{\hspace{2cm}}$

(b) $y = \dfrac{ax + b}{c}$

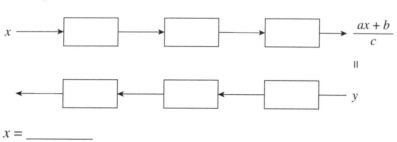

$x = \underline{\hspace{2cm}}$

(c) $y = a(x + b) - d$

$x \longrightarrow$

(d) $y = \dfrac{2}{3}ax^2$

(e) $y = \pi x^2 h$

10.9 Inequalities

1 Solve these linear inequalities. The first one has been done for you.

(a) $3x + 2 > 17$

    (2) $3x > 15$

    (÷3) $x > 5$

(b) $5x + 2 > 27$

    (−2)

    (÷5)

(c) $4x - 2 < 14$

> **I can do this page!**

> **Remember**
>
> Solving a linear inequality is very similar to solving linear equations.

(d) $6x - 4 < 26$

(e) $7x + 3 > 21$

(f) $5x - 9 < 36$

2 Show the solution sets to these inequalities on a number line.

(a) $x \geqslant 2$

(b) $x < 2$

(c) $x \leqslant -1$

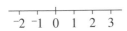

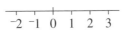

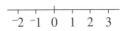

3 Solve these linear inequalities and show their solution sets on a number line.

(a) $3x + 4 < 7$

(b) $6x - 4 \geqslant 8$

(c) $8x + 2 \leqslant -14$

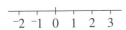

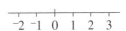

4 Solve these linear inequalities:

(a) $3x + 4 < 2x + 8$

(b) $5x - 3 > 4x + 5$

(c) $7x - 3 < 5x + 5$

(d) $3(x + 3) > x + 27$

(e) $5(3x - 4) > 8x + 1$

(f) $\dfrac{4(x - 2)}{3} < x$

I can do
this page!

(g) $6(x - 3) - 4 \geqslant 5x + 4$

(h) $3(3 - 2x) + 4x \leqslant 6 - 4x$

5 The area of a rectangular field is less than $1500\,\text{m}^2$. What is the width of the field if its length is $50\,\text{m}$?

6 The perimeter of a rectangle is less than $30\,\text{cm}$. The length of the rectangle is $5\,\text{cm}$ longer than its width, w.

(a) Form an inequality in w for the perimeter of the rectangle.

(b) Solve the inequality to find the length and width of the rectangle.

7* A store sells black ink pens for $5 and red ink pens for $4. Kerwin wishes to buy 20 pens but he has no more than $92.

(a) Writing r for the number of red pens, form an inequality to show this information

(b) Solve the inequality and find the least number of red pens he can buy.

Volume

11.1 Volume

1 What is the volume of these shapes?

(a)

Volume = _____ cubes

(b)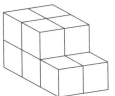

Volume = _____ cubes

(c)

Volume = _____ cubes

I can do
this page!

> **Remember**
>
>
>
> Volume is measured in cubic centimetres, cm³.
>
> Volume is $1\,cm \times 1\,cm \times 1\,cm = 1\,cm^3$

2 Write down an item that has a volume of about:

(a) $1\,cm^3$ _____

(b) $5\,cm^3$ _____

(c) $100\,cm^3$ _____

(d) $500\,cm^3$ _____

3 **(a)** How big is the average mouse?

(b) If you put a mouse in a box, about how big would the box need to be?

Length _____ cm   Width _____ cm   Height _____ cm

4

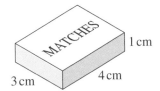

(a) How many centimetre cubes could you fit into a matchbox 4 cm long,
3 cm wide and 1 cm high? _____

(b) How many such match boxes could fit into a box with dimensions
8 cm by 6 cm by 2 cm? _____

11.2 Volume of cuboids

1 A   B 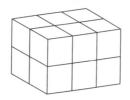   C 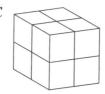   D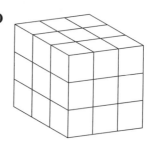

I can do
this page!

(a) Complete the table.

Shape	No. cubes long (l)	No. cubes wide (w)	No. cubes height (h)	$l \times w \times h$	Volume V
A	2	1	2	$2 \times 1 \times 2$	
B		2			
C			2		
D					

(b) Complete: Volume of a cuboid, $V =$

2 Find the volume of these cuboids

(a)

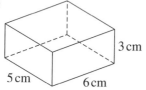

3 cm

5 cm   6 cm

Volume =

(b)

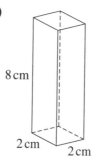

8 cm

2 cm   2 cm

Volume =

(c)

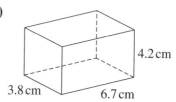

4.2 cm

3.8 cm   6.7 cm

Volume =

3 Complete the table for cuboids with the dimensions given.

Length (m)	2	3	15	12	8	7.2	7	
Width (m)	1	7	8	4		6.8	3	14
Height (m)	5	9	12		2	10		6.1
Volume (m³)				144	216		35	170.8

4 **(a)** What is the volume of a cube with side length 8 cm? _____

(b) What is the volume of a cube with side length 16 cm? _____

(c) How many cubes with side 8 cm could fit into a cube with side length 16 cm? _____

11.3 Volumes of prisms and cylinders

Remember

Any solid shape with a constant cross-section

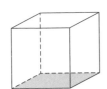 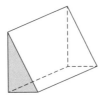 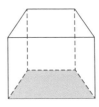

has volume, V, given by the formula

$V = A \times h$ where A is area of cross-section and h is height

I can do
this page!

1 Find the area of the cross-section and volume of these cuboids.

(a)
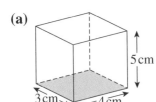

Area = _____

Volume = _____

(b)
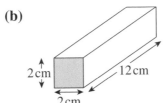

Area = _____

Volume = _____

(c)
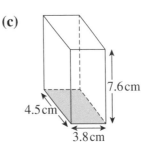

Area = _____

Volume = _____

2 Find the area of cross-section and volume of these prisms.

(a)
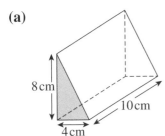

Area = _____

Volume = _____

(b)
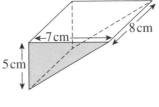

Area = _____

Volume = _____

(c)
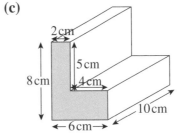

Area = _____

Volume = _____

3 Find the area of cross-section and volume of these cylinders.

(a)
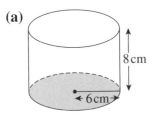

Area = _____

Volume = _____

(b)
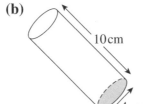

Area = _____

Volume = _____

(c)
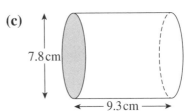

Area = _____

Volume = _____

11.4 Volume of liquids

1 Estimate the volume in ml of:

(a) a tablespoon of liquid   _____ ml

(b) a teacup of hot chocolate   _____ ml

(c) a large glass of juice   _____ ml

(d) a large tin of evaporated milk   _____ ml

(e) a large tube of toothpaste   _____ ml

> **Remember**
>
> A container with a volume of $1000\,cm^3$ can hold 1 litre of liquid.
>
> 1 litre = $1000\,cm^3$
>
> 1 ml = $1\,cm^3$,
>
> where ml is a millilitre.

I can do this page!

2 Find the capacity in litres of containers with volume:

(a) $10\,000\,cm^3$ _____

(b) $35\,000\,cm^3$ _____

(c) $800\,cm^3$ _____

(d) $125\,cm^3$ _____

3 A water tank is built in the shape of a cuboid with a square base, side 1 m and height 2 m.

(a) What is the volume of the tank in cubic metres (m^3)?

(b) What is the volume of the tank in cm^3?

(c) How many litres of water will the tank hold when full?

4 A tin has the shape of a cuboid. It can hold 120 ml of liquid. What could be the dimensions of the tin? Give three solutions.

(i) _____

(ii) _____

(iii) _____

11.5 Surface area of solids

1 Find the area of each of the marked faces of the solids.
Hence, find the surface area of the solid.

I can do this page!

(a)

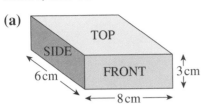

Area FRONT = _____

Area SIDE = _____

Area TOP = _____

Total surface area = _____

(b)

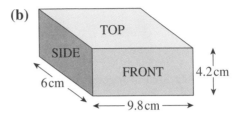

Area FRONT = _____

Area SIDE = _____

Area TOP = _____

Total surface area = _____

2 Find the total surface area of a cube with side:

(a) 6 cm

_____

(b) 3.8 cm

_____

3 Find the total surface area of these triangular prisms:

(a)

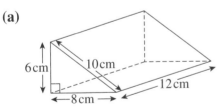

Area of back = _____

Area of bottom = _____

Area of top = _____

Area of triangular side = _____

Total surface area = _____

(b)

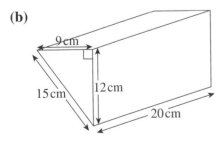

Area of back = _____

Area of bottom = _____

Area of top = _____

Area of triangular side = _____

Total surface area = _____

(c)

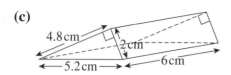

Total surface area =   _____

4   Find the curved surface area of these cylinders:

(a)

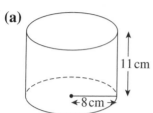

(b)

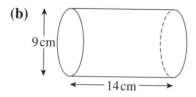

Curved surface area =   Curved surface area =

= _____   = _____

5   A can of kidney beans has diameter 10 cm and height 15 cm.

(a) What is the area of its base?

_____

(b) What is its curved surface area?

_____

(c) Calculate the area of tin needed to make the can.

_____

6   A box of chocolates with dimensions 20 cm × 10 cm × 24 cm is gift wrapped using a sheet of wrapping paper 1m by 2 m.

(a) Find the surface area of the box.

_____

(b) Is there sufficient wrapping paper to gift wrap the box of chocolates?
Give reasons for your answer.

_____

Consumer arithmetic (12)

12.1 Banking 1

1 State two ways in which **savings accounts** differ from **chequing accounts**.

(i) _____

(ii) _____

✓ I can do this page!

2 Complete this cheque to J. R. Robinson for $843.17.

	1383
	DATE: ....../....../20......
PAY TO THE ORDER OF	$ [ ]
....	
.... DOLLARS	
FOR..	....

ιΟιιΟ ιƷθι ΟΟ9ᄔᄔ θι9Ο ιƷθƷ

3 Complete Albert's pass book for his savings accounts.

Date	Reference	Withdrawal ($)	Deposit ($)	Balance ($)
6/5				3142.47
8/5	cash	500		
12/5	cheque		423.84	
18/5	cheque		713.63	
21/5	cheque			4304.15
30/5	cheque	38.95		

4 (a) What bank or credit union does your family use to keep their money in? _____

(b) What is the interest rate for savings accounts? _____

(c) What is the interest rate for chequing accounts? _____

> **Remember**
>
> **Interest** is the fee paid by the bank for the use of the money you deposit there.

12.2 Banking 2

1   What is a debit card?

I can do
this page!

_____

2   What is a credit card?

_____

3   Write down *two* ways in which a debit card differs from a credit card.

(i) _____

(ii) _____

4   **(a)** Go to some local banks or search online. Find the name of three different
       credit cards and find their interest rates to complete the table.

Name of credit card	Interest rate

(b) How long can you wait before you have to pay interest? _____

(c) What happens if you fail to pay back the bank? _____

5   Go to your local bank or credit union.

(a) What debit card is used? _____

(b) What fees are associated with the use of this card? _____

(c) Is there a limit on the amount that can be borrowed on any one day?

       If so, what is it? _____

12.3 Using percentages

1 Write these percentages as fractions in their
simplest form.

(a) 25% =   (b) 65% =

(c) 80% =   (d) 34% =

(e) 16% =   (f) $87\frac{1}{2}\% =$

Remember

12% means

'12 out of 100' or $\frac{12}{100} = \frac{3}{25}$

I can do
this page!

2 Write these fractions as percentages. The first one has
been done for you.

(a) $\frac{4}{5} = \frac{4}{5} \times 100\% = \frac{400}{5}\% = 80\%$ (b) $\frac{3}{5} =$

(c) $\frac{11}{20} =$ (d) $\frac{3}{25} =$

(e) $\frac{3}{12} =$ (f) $\frac{3}{8} =$

3 Complete the table.

Fraction	Percentage
$\frac{3}{4}$	$\frac{3}{4} \times 100\% = 3 \times 25\% = 75\%$
$\frac{2}{5}$	
	35%
$\frac{7}{12}$	
	88%

4 Find the percentage of these amounts. The first one has been done for you.

(a) 5% of $60 = $\frac{5}{100} \times \$60 = \$\frac{30}{10} = \$3$ (b) 10% of $305 =

(c) 15% of $4000 =   (d) 4% of $75 =

(e) 9% of $420 =   (f) 20% of $73.50 =

12.4 Simple interest

1   Alsana has $600 in her bank. The bank pays interest of 3% each year.

    (a) How much interest does Alsana get after one year?

    (b) After 3 years?   _____

    (c) After 8 years?   _____

    (d) How much money will she have in the bank after 8 years?

                                         _____

I can do
this page!

2   The interest rate at Brown's Bank is 4%. How much interest is earned on

    (a) $8000 for one year   _____

    (b) $500 for one year   _____

    (c) $500 for three years?   _____

3   Find the interest on these loans:

    (a) $500 for 2 years at 8%

                        Interest = _____

    (b) $12 000 for 8 years at 10%

                        Interest = _____

    (c) $2850 for 4 years at 11%

                        Interest = _____

4   Lana deposits $4000 in her Credit Union that gives 5% simple interest. How long does she need to wait before she has $5000?

5   What is the rate of interest at a bank if a deposit of $100 takes 20 years to double in value?

12.5 Compound interest

1 **(a)** What is **compound** interest?

_____

I can do
this page!

(b) How does compound interest differ from simple interest?

_____

2 A bank gives compound interest at a rate of 2% per annum.

(a) What is the interest on $1000 after 1 year?

_____

(b) What is the principal after 1 year?

_____

(c) What is the interest for the second year?

_____

(d) What is the total compound interest after two years?

_____

3 Find the compound interest on:

(a) $15 000 for 2 years at 4%

_____

(b) $18 000 for 2 years at 5%

_____

(c) $20 000 for 3 years at 2%

_____

4 **(a)** Calculate the compound interest on a loan of $15 000 taken for a period of two years if the interest rate is 8%.

_____

(b) How much money should be repaid each month?

_____

12.6 Taxes

1 Value added tax (VAT) is 15%. Find the sale price of these items with the prices shown.

I can do
this page!

(a)

(b)

$120

VAT = _____

Sale price= _____

$4500

VAT = _____

Sale price = _____

2 Complete the table.

Item	Price before tax ($)	Tax	Rate	Total tax ($)	Sale price
Notebook	2500	Sales	8%		
Stove	1800	VAT	15%		
Cell phone	780	GCT	16.5%		
Bicycle	1600	Consumption	20%		
Toaster		Sales	10%	$60	

3 Find out about tax rates in your country.

(a) How much must you earn before you have to pay income tax? _____

(b) What are the income tax rates? _____

4 The tax rate and allowances in a certain country are as follows.

Tax-free allowance	Tax rate
$40 000	30%

Remember

Income tax is the tax paid to the government on money you earn.

Income that is not taxed is called **tax-free** income. Income that is taxed is called **taxable** or **chargeable** income.

(a) Stefan earns $100 000 each year.

(i) What is his chargeable income? _____

(ii) How much income tax does he pay? _____

(iii) What is his net annual income? _____

(b) Shani earns $38 560 each year.

(i) What is her chargeable income? _____

(ii) How much income tax does she pay? _____

12.7 Hire purchase

Remember

Hire purchase is a way of buying goods by paying instalments over time.
Often the customer will first make a deposit.

I can do
this page!

1

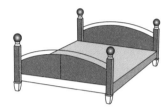

Deposit $500
Monthly payment $400

Deposit $300
Monthly payment $250

Find the hire purchase price for the items shown, if payments are to be made for 2 years.

(a) Bed deposit   = _____

     Total instalments   = _____

     Hire purchase price   = _____

(b) Armchair deposit   = _____

     Total instalments   = _____

     Hire purchase price   = _____

2

Cash $5600
Deposit 10%
24 monthly payments
of $300

Cash $2100
Deposit 5%
52 weekly payments
of $40

(a) Find the hire purchase price of the items shown.

     (i) Computer deposit   = _____

        Total instalments   = _____

        Hire purchase price   = _____

     (ii) Microwave deposit   = _____

        Total instalments   = _____

        Hire purchase price   = _____

(b) In each case, how much would you save if you paid cash?

     (i) Computer saving   = _____

     (ii) Microwave saving   = _____

3* Find the hire purchase price of a bicycle that has a $1600 cash price, if the deposit is 15% and
weekly instalments of $20 must be paid for two years.

_____

Multiple choice 4

In each question, circle the correct answer.

1 What is the 27th odd number?

   A 27   **B** 53   **C** 55   **D** 57

2 A total of *A* adults and *C* children go to a show. Adult tickets cost $10 while children's tickets are $5. What is the cost of all the tickets?

   A $15*AC*   **B** $(5*A* + 10*C*)

   C $(10*A* + 5*C*)   **D** $15(*A* + *C*)

3 What is $3p - 2q - 5p + 7q$ in its simplest form?

   A $^-2p + 5q$ **B** $2p + 5q$ **C** $2p + 9q$ **D** $^-2p + 9q$

4

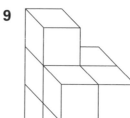

The perimeter of the shape is:

   A $6a + b$ **B** $7a + b$

   B $8a + b$ **C** $9a + b$

5 What is the solution to the equation $\frac{x}{3} + 4 = 7$?

   A $x = 3$ **B** $x = 6$ **C** $x = 9$ **D** $x = 12$

6 Andrew has three times as many marbles as Jim. Altogether they have 32 marbles. How many marbles has Jim?

   A 8   **B** 16   **C** 24   **D** 30

7

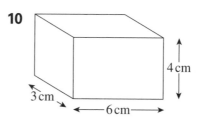

The diagram shows the solution set to which inequality?

   A $x + 3 < 2$ **B** $x - 2 > ^-1$

   C $2x > 3 - x$ **D** $2x < 1 + x$

8 When rewritten, the formula
$v = u + at$
is

I can do this page!

   A $t = \dfrac{v + u}{a}$ **B** $t = \dfrac{v}{a} - u$

   C $t = v - \dfrac{u}{a}$ **D** $t = \dfrac{v - u}{a}$

9

The solid above is made from 1 cm³ cubes. What is its volume?

   A 4 cm³   **B** 8 cm²

   C 9 cm³   **D** 14 cm³

10

A cuboid has dimensions 6 cm by 3 cm by 4 cm. What is its volume?

   A 13 cm³   **B** 24 cm³

   C 72 cm³   **D** 144 cm³

11 A cube has a volume of 125 cm³. What is the area of one of its faces?

   A 5 cm²   **B** 20 cm²

   C 25 cm²   **D** 100 cm²

12 A water container has a volume of 2 m³. How many litres of water does it hold?

   A 2   **B** 200   **C** 2000   **D** 20 000

13

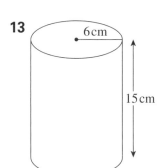

A cylindrical tin has radius 6 cm and height 15 cm. What is the volume of the tin?

A $90\pi\,cm^3$ 　　　　B $18\pi\,cm^3$

C $360\pi\,cm^3$ 　　　　D $540\pi\,cm^3$

14 A wooden pencil case has the form of a cuboid and has a base area of $120\,cm^2$. What is its height if the volume of the case is $600\,cm^3$?

A 4 cm　　B 5 cm　　C 6 cm　　D 8 cm

15 What is the surface area of a box with dimensions 10 cm by 8 cm by 4 cm?

A $152\,cm^2$ 　　　　B $160\,cm^2$

C $304\,cm^2$ 　　　　D $320\,cm^2$

16 One disadvantage of using a credit card is:

A it takes a long time to make transactions

B it is easy to make transaction errors

C money is transferred immediately from your account

D delayed payment results in high interest payments

17 What is the simple interest charged on a loan of $5000 when borrowed from a bank which has an interest rate of 10% for a period of 4 years?

A $50 　　　　　　B $200

C $500 　　　　　　D $2000

I can do this page!

18 The tax-free allowance in Jamaica is $60 000. How much tax does Desmond pay on an annual salary of $100 000 if the tax rate on chargeable income is 25%?

A $10 000　　B $15 000

C $25 000　　D $40 000

19 A ring is priced at $20 000. What is the sale price of this ring if there is a 15% sales tax?

A $3000 　　　　　B $17 000

C $23 000 　　　　D $50 000

20 What is the hire purchase price of a stove that has a cash price of $2000 and can be bought on hire purchase for a 20% deposit and 24 monthly payments of $90?

A $2160　B $2200　C $2400　D $2560

Check your answers in the back of the book:

Score = /20

Answers

1.1
1 (a) $\frac{5}{12}$ (b) $\frac{7}{16}$ (c) $\frac{7}{12}$ (d) $\frac{6}{16}$

2 (a) $\frac{10}{15}$ (b) $\frac{18}{24}$ (c) $\frac{20}{32}$ (d) $\frac{15}{35}$ (e) $\frac{5}{80}$

   (f) $\frac{63}{72}$ (g) $\frac{65}{78}$ (h) $\frac{30}{102}$

3 (b) $\frac{6}{7}$ (c) $\frac{2}{3}$ (d) $\frac{7}{16}$ (e) $\frac{1}{6}$ (f) $\frac{3}{7}$

4 (a) $\frac{5}{2}$ (b) $\frac{11}{3}$ (c) $\frac{31}{8}$ (d) $\frac{27}{5}$ (e) $\frac{79}{10}$ (f) $\frac{69}{16}$

5 (a) $2\frac{4}{7}$ (b) $8\frac{1}{4}$ (c) $3\frac{1}{5}$ (d) $5\frac{3}{7}$ (e) $9\frac{2}{5}$ (f) $15\frac{3}{4}$

6 (a) $1\frac{1}{4}$ (b) $1\frac{4}{9}$ (c) $2\frac{2}{3}$ (d) 2

1.2
1 (a) $\frac{9}{10}$ (b) $1\frac{1}{8}$ (c) $1\frac{8}{21}$ (d) $1\frac{13}{44}$

   (e) $\frac{31}{36}$ (f) $\frac{11}{13}$ (g) $1\frac{1}{30}$ (h) $1\frac{22}{75}$

2 (b) $6\frac{1}{12}$ (c) $7\frac{3}{8}$ (d) $4\frac{23}{35}$ (e) $8\frac{1}{8}$

3 (a) $\frac{1}{8}$ (b) $\frac{1}{2}$ (c) $\frac{1}{21}$ (d) $\frac{1}{12}$

   (e) $\frac{17}{63}$ (f) $\frac{17}{44}$ (g) $\frac{1}{104}$ (h) $\frac{41}{153}$

4 $6\frac{5}{8}$ km

5 (a) $\frac{7}{12}$ gallon (b) 5 gallons

1.3
1 (a) $\frac{3}{8}$ (b) $\frac{1}{2}$ (c) $\frac{9}{16}$ (d) $\frac{5}{12}$

2 (a) $\frac{1}{3}$ (b) $\frac{1}{6}$ (c) $\frac{1}{4}$ (d) $\frac{7}{30}$

   (e) $\frac{4}{21}$ (f) $\frac{3}{20}$ (g) $\frac{3}{16}$ (h) $\frac{1}{19}$

3 (b) $7\frac{19}{40}$ (c) $15\frac{5}{8}$ (d) $26\frac{2}{15}$ (e) $17\frac{1}{9}$

4 (a) 6 (b) 5 (c) 2

6 (a) $2\frac{2}{5}$ (b) $2\frac{1}{2}$ (c) $1\frac{2}{7}$ (d) $2\frac{1}{4}$

   (e) $1\frac{1}{6}$ (f) $\frac{1}{3}$ (g) $4\frac{1}{2}$ (h) $\frac{7}{12}$

7 (b) $1\frac{1}{2}$ (c) $2\frac{4}{9}$ (d) $1\frac{89}{95}$ (e) $1\frac{19}{22}$

8 $\frac{10}{13}$ 9 (a) $3\frac{2}{3}$ km (b) 15

10 $18\frac{6}{13}$ (18 complete pieces)

1.4
1 (a) 5:1 (b) 5:13 (c) 4:1 (d) 1:3 (e) 4:3 (f) 8:9

2 (a) \$90, \$30 (b) \$75, \$45 (c) \$36, \$84 (d) \$95, \$25

3 (a) 160 (b) 276 (c) 190

4 (a) \$12, \$18, \$30 (b) \$100, \$225, \$300

   (c) 6, 15, 36

6 \$98

1.5
1

2^5	2^4	2^3	2^2	2^1	2^0	Number
		1	0	1	1	10
		1	1	0	1	14
	1	0	1	1	1	23
1	0	1	0	1	0	42
1	1	0	1	0	1	53

2 (a) 15 (b) 22 (c) 46 (d) 126

3 (a) 10 000 (b) 1100 (c) 11 000 (d) 11 110

4

5^3	5^2	5^1	5^0	Number
	1	3	4	44
	4	2	3	113
3	0	4	4	399
4	1	2	2	637

5 (a) 22 (b) 40 (c) 101 (d) 440

6 (a) 100 (b) 324

2.1
2 A = 2.9 B = 3.15 C = 3.42 D = 3.6

   E = 3.88 F = 4.05

3 (a) 0.073 (b) 0.084 (c) 0.3

6 (a) 2m boy (b) 0.18 m

2.2
1 (a) 29.72 (b) 5.21 (c) 214.52 (d) 11.053

2 (a) 14.36 (b) 1.42 (c) 182.353

3 0.24 m

4 1.21 s

5 (a) 205.81 g (b) 44.19 g

6 (a) 44.75 (b) 132.52 (c) 8.003

2.3
1 (a) 36 (b) 1740 (c) 6.8 (d) 0.342

   (e) 1130 (f) 0.495 (g) 4.2 (h) 0.803

   (i) 606

2 (a) 1000 (b) 100 (c) 1000 (d) 789.5

   (e) 0.073 (f) 952

3 (a) 25.86 (b) 258.6 (c) 2.586 (d) 2.586

   (e) 0.2586 (f) 258.6

4 (a) 8.28 (b) 3.108 (c) 136.84 (d) 0.4536

2.4
1 (b) 1.06 (c) 6.25 (d) 0.008 (e) 0.483

   (f) 0.0789

2 (a) $13.42   (b) $174.46

3 (b) 410   (c) 7.5

4 (a) $8.37\,\text{ms}^{-1}$ (b) 54.2 m

2.5

1 (a) 196   (b) 289   (c) 576   (d) 7569

2 (a) 9   (b) 27   (c) 36   (d) 52

5 174.4 m

6 10201

2.6

1 (a) 1.4   (b) 2.5   (c) 17.9

2 (a) 1.6   (b) 3.1   (c) 2.8   (d) 3.2   (e) 2.6

   (f) 1.3   (g) 2.1   (h) 1.1   (i) 3.0

3 (a) 1.29   (b) 6.91   (c) 4.22   (d) 8.92   (e) 14.33

   (f) 0.03   (g) 0.72   (h) 0.21   (i) 0.84

2.7

1 (a) 30   (b) 60   (c) 60   (d) 70

2 (a) 60   (b) 60   (c) 20   (d) 10

3

Number	8245	2036	4893	11932	306469
3 s.f	8250	2040	4890	11900	306000
2 s.f	8200	2000	4900	12000	310000
1 s.f	8000	2000	5000	10000	300000

4 (a) 4   (b) 0.7   (c) 0.008   (d) 20

5

Number	0.8462	0.01698	0.4164	0.008947	0.00006246
3 s.f	0.846	0.0170	0.416	0.00895	0.0000625
2 s.f	0.85	0.017	0.42	0.0089	0.000062
1 s.f	0.8	0.02	0.4	0.009	0.00006

6 (a) $64999   (b) $54000

7 (a) 500000   (b) 0.03   (c) 80000

2.8

1 (a) 1000   (b) 8.9   (c) 4.3

   (d) 7.2   (e) 2.94   (f) 6.934

2 (a) 30000   (b) 370   (c) 18500

   (d) 280000   (e) 7680   (f) 4090000

3 (a) 9×10^3 (b) 7.6×10^3 (c) 8.9×10^2

   (d) 7.4×10 (e) 1.46×10^3 (f) 3.36×10^4

   (g) 81.6×10 (h) 2.1294×10^2 (i) 6.0361×10^2

   (j) 7.3604×10^4

4 (a) 5.98×10, 63, 6×10^2, 602, 4×10^3

   (b) 1.9×10^3, 2000, 2.1×10^3, 3164, 1.8×10^4

5 (a) $2.697\,983 \times 10^6$ (b) 2788334

6 496.56, 4.9656×10^2

2.9

1 (a) $\dfrac{3}{10}$ (b) $\dfrac{7}{20}$ (c) $\dfrac{23}{50}$ (d) $\dfrac{3}{8}$

   (e) $\dfrac{1}{16}$ (f) $\dfrac{7}{16}$

2 (b) 0.625   (c) 0.44…   (d) 0.4166…   (e) 0.833…

3 (a) 0.286   (b) 0.385   (c) 0.786   (d) 0.235

   (e) 0.923   (f) 0.273

4 (a) $\dfrac{1}{9}$ (b) $\dfrac{1}{11}$ (c) $\dfrac{5}{11}$ (d) $\dfrac{5}{12}$

3.2

5 (b) AC = 13 cm

3.3

1 (a) 138°   (b) 62°   (c) 59°

2 (a) 47°, 133°   (b) 132°, 48°, 97°

3 (a) 96°   (b) 76°   (c) 71°

4 (a) 60°   (b) 60°   (c) 110°

3.4

2 (a) 64°   (b) 29°   (c) 73°

4 (a) 134°   (b) 107°   (c) 55°

3.5

3 (a) 47°, 47°   (b) 124°, 56°   (c) 117°, 63°

   (d) 48°, 48°, 132°   (e) 37°, 143°   (f) 25°, 30°

4 (a) 130°, 70°   (b) 128°, 52°   (c) 46°, 141°

   (d) 52°, 52°   (e) 109°, 63°   (f) 121°, 49°

   (g) 65°, 115°   (h) 120°, 70°   (i) 70°, 123°

Multiple choice 1

1 A   **2** D   **3** D   **4** B   **5** A   **6** C   **7** C

8 A   **9** C   **10** C   **11** B   **12** C   **13** B   **14** B

15 D   **16** C   **17** C   **18** C   **19** C   **20** B

4.1

1 (a) (i) Al, Kelly, Susan, Jones, David

   (ii) Al, Susan, Omar, Rasheed, Chad, Alex

   (iii) Al, Susan

   (b) (i) Samantha, Chris, Sean, Nicole, Ashley, Courtney

   (ii) Samantha, Chris, Sean, Romario, Sheldon, Andre

   (iii) Samantha, Chris, Sean

2 (a) {2, 4}   (b) {14, 28}   (c) { }   (d) {1, 2, 4, 8}

   (e) {3, 6, 12, 15, 30, 60}

3 (b) {7, 11}

4.2

1 (a) {1, 2, 3, 4, 6, 8}   (b) {4, 6, 14, 16, 36, 46}

   (c) {a, b, c, d, e, f, g}   (d) {1, 2, 4, 5, 8, 10}

   (e) {1, 2, 4, 8, 12, 16, 20}

2 **(a)** **(i)** {1, 3, 5, 6, 7, 9, 11, 13, 15, 17, 19}

  (ii) {1, 3, 9, 18}

 (b) **(i)** {1, 2, 4, 6, 7, 8, 10, 12, 14, 16, 18, 20, 22, 24, 26, 28}

  (ii) {2, 4, 14}

3 **(a)** **(ii)** {1, 2, 3, 4, 6, 9, 12, 18, 36}

 (b) **(ii)** {2, 4, 6, 8, 10, 12, 14, 16, 18, 20, 22, 24, 26, 28, 30}

4.3

1 **(a)** {1, 3, 5, 7, 9, 11, 13, 15, 16, 17, 18, 19, 20}

 (b) {4, 5, 7, 8, 10, 11, 12, 13, 14, 15, 16, 17, 19, 20}

 (c) {1, 2, 3, 5, 6, 7, 9, 10, 11, 13, 14, 15, 17, 18, 19}

 (d) {1, 2, 3, 5, 7, 11, 13, 17, 19}

 (e) {1, 17, 18, 19, 20}

2 **(a)** Elephants with small ears

 (b) Composite numbers

 (c) Coffee beans that are not Blue Mountain

3 **(a)** **(i)** {3, 5, 6, 7, 9, 10, 11, 12, 13, 14, 15, 17, 18, 19, 20}

  (ii) {2, 4, 6, 8, 10, 12, 14, 16, 18, 20}

  (iii) {Whole numbers 2 – 20}

 (b) **(i)** {large, fierce dogs}

  (ii) {timid dogs}

  (iii) {dogs that are not large or fierce}

5.1

1 **(a)** km **(b)** g **(c)** mm **(d)** kg **(e)** cm

5.2

1 **(a)** 20 cm **(b)** 16.5 cm **(c)** 39 cm

2 **(a)** 31.4 cm **(b)** 52.75 cm

3 **(a)** 13.4 cm **(b)** 1.7 cm

4 **(a)** 43.96 cm **(b)** 23.13 cm **(c)** 41.12 cm **(d)** 30.47 cm

5.3

1 **(a)** 32 cm² **(b)** 12.6 cm² **(c)** 40.96 cm²

2 **(b)** 18 cm² **(c)** 42 cm²

3 **(b)** 42 cm² **(c)** 44.52 cm²

4 4 cm

5 **(a)** 40 cm² **(b)** 24 cm² **(c)** 64 cm²

6 **(a)** 6 cm², 8 cm², 9 cm², 4 cm², 29 cm²

 (b) 30 cm², 14 cm², 15 cm², 41 cm²

7 **(a)** 56 cm² **(b)** 92 cm² **(c)** 67.5 cm²

 (d) 44 cm² **(e)** 104.5 cm²

5.4

2 **(a)** 78.5 cm² **(b)** 162.8 cm² **(c)** 113.04 cm²

 (d) 171.9 cm²

3 **(a)** 100.5 cm² **(b)** 15.9 cm² **(c)** 115.4 cm²

5.5

2 **(a)** **(i)** 5.7 cm **(ii)** 6.4 cm **(iii)** 6 cm

 (b) **(i)** 34.2 km **(ii)** 38.4 km **(iii)** 36 km

3 **(b)** 1:500 **(c)** 1:200 000 **(d)** 1:4 000 000

6.1

1 **(a)** ⁻2 **(b)** ⁻1 **(c)** 0 **(d)** 3 **(e)** ⁻7 **(f)** ⁻8

 (g) ⁻5 **(h)** 3 **(i)** ⁻4

2 **(a)** ⁻9 **(b)** 2 **(c)** ⁻8 **(d)** ⁻3 **(e)** 2 **(f)** ⁻2

 (g) ⁻7 **(h)** ⁻6 **(i)** ⁻11

4 **(a)** ⁻1, 1, 3, 5 **(b)** ⁻18, ⁻22, ⁻26, ⁻30 **(c)** ⁻1, 4, 9, 14

6.2

1 **(c)** adding

2 **(a)** 9 **(b)** 9 **(c)** 8 **(d)** 2 **(e)** ⁻2 **(f)** 21

 (g) 27 **(h)** ⁻2 **(i)** ⁻7 **(j)** 41

4 8°C

5 8714 feet

7 **(a)** ⁻2 **(b)** ⁻3 **(c)** 4 **(d)** ⁻3 **(e)** ⁻3 **(f)** 12

9 **(a)** ⁻2 **(b)** ⁻3 **(c)** 3 **(d)** ⁻2 **(e)** 3

 (f) ⁻3 **(g)** ⁻6 **(h)** 6 **(i)** ⁻7

6.3

1 **(a)** ⁻12 **(b)** ⁻12 **(c)** ⁻15 **(d)** ⁻32 **(e)** ⁻45

2 **(a)** ⁻15 **(b)** ⁻28 **(c)** ⁻24 **(d)** ⁻24 **(e)** ⁻24 **(f)** ⁻24

 (g) ⁻12 **(h)** ⁻21 **(i)** ⁻48

3 **(c)** positive

4 **(a)** 12 **(b)** ⁻12 **(c)** 12 **(d)** ⁻30 **(e)** 30 **(f)** 30

 (g) 21 **(h)** ⁻21

5 **(a)** ⁻2 **(b)** 4 **(c)** ⁻3 **(d)** ⁻6 **(e)** 4 **(f)** ⁻9

 (g) ⁻4 **(h)** 8 **(i)** ⁻6

7 **(a)** ⁻2 **(b)** ⁻3 **(c)** 4 **(d)** ⁻3 **(e)** ⁻3 **(f)** 12

8 **(a)** negative **(b)** positive

9 **(a)** ⁻2 **(b)** ⁻3 **(c)** 3 **(d)** ⁻2 **(e)** 3 **(f)** ⁻3

 (g) ⁻6 **(h)** 6 **(i)** ⁻7

Multiple choice 2

1 C **2** A **3** D **4** A **5** A **6** C **7** C

8 D **9** C **10** D **11** C **12** B **13** D **14** B

15 B **16** A **17** B **18** B **19** B **20** A

7.1

3 **(a)** $x \rightarrow x + 2$ **(b)** $x \rightarrow 3x$ **(c)** $x \rightarrow 5x + 1$

7.2

3 **(a)** $y = x + 3$ **(b)** $y = 2x + 2$ **(c)** $y = 5 - x$

7.3

1 (a) 1 mm   (b) Saturday   (c) Wednesday

2 (a) $15   (b) 5 m   (c) $12.50

3 (a) week 2   (b) 25 cm   (c) after week 7

   (d) during week 4

4 (a) 9 cm   (b) 3   (c) 6.5 cm

5 (b) (i) $11\frac{1}{2}$ (ii) 152.5 cm

6 (b) 28.5°   (c) 7.30 am and 5 pm

7 (b) (i) 38.47 cm²   (ii) 3.6 cm

7.4

1 (c) (0, 2), (1, 5), (2, 8), (3, 11), (4, 14)

2 (c) $5\frac{1}{2}$ **3** (c) ⁻2   **4** (c) $2\frac{2}{3}$

5 (c) $3\frac{1}{2}$ **6** (c) $-2\frac{1}{2}$ **7** (c) (4, 7)

7.5

1 (a) 1, ⁻1   (b) $\frac{1}{2}$, 2

2 (a) 2, ⁻3   (b) 4, 2   (c) 5, ⁻9

4 (a) (⁻1, 0), (1, 4)   (b) 2   (c) $y = 2x + 2$

7.6

3 (a) $x > 2$ (b) $x < 5$ (c) $y < 3$ (d) $y > ⁻2$

8.1

3 (b) (1, ⁻2), (4, ⁻2), (4, ⁻4)   (d) (⁻1, ⁻2), (⁻4, ⁻2), (⁻4, ⁻4)

4 (a) (4, 1), (3, ⁻3), (2, 0)

8.2

1 (b) 6 right, 0 down   (c) 8 right, 3 up

   (d) 2 left, 3 up   (e) 2 left, 3 up

   (e) 3 left, 2 down   (f) 8 left, 3 up

3 (b) (0, ⁻2), (2, 1), (3, ⁻2)

4 (d) 2 right, 2 up

8.3

1 (a) $\begin{pmatrix}5\\2\end{pmatrix}$ (b) $\begin{pmatrix}⁻2\\4\end{pmatrix}$ (c) $\begin{pmatrix}⁻3\\⁻4\end{pmatrix}$

3 (a) $\begin{pmatrix}2\\1\end{pmatrix}$ (b) $\begin{pmatrix}⁻2\\1\end{pmatrix}$ (c) $\begin{pmatrix}⁻4\\1\end{pmatrix}$

8.4

2 (a) 2   (b) 4   (c) 5   (d) 8

   (e) 6   (f) 0   (g) 0   (h) 3

9.1

1 (b) 7

2 (a) 15   (b) 55   (c) 20

3 (a) 10   (b) 40   (c) 110

5 (c) 41 – 45 s

9.2

1 (a) 10°   (b) 70°

2 (a) 3°

3 (a) 240

5 (a) 4°   (b) 30   (c) 5

6 (a) 4000   (b) 2500

9.3

1 (a) 75°F   (b) July   (c) April, October   (d) 67°F

3 (d) 13

9.4

1 (a) 5   (b) 7   (c) 91.5

2 (a) 25.4°   (b) 25°   (c) 25°

3 (a) 8   (c) 8   (d) 7.3

4 (a) 30 g   (b) 30.5 g   (c) 31.8 g

5 (a) 25   (b) 0   (c) 1   (d) 1.36

Multiple choice 3

1 D   **2** D   **3** C   **4** B   **5** C   **6** A   **7** C

8 A   **9** B   **10** A   **11** B   **12** A   **13** A   **14** C

15 C   **16** B   **17** D   **18** A   **19** D   **20** C

10.1

3 (c) 400

10.2

1 (c) 120

10.3

1 (a) 36   (b) 105   (c) 5050

2 (a) 18 feet   (b) 18 yards

3 (a) 95°F   (b) 183.2°F

4 (a) 50.24 cm²   (b) 136.8 cm²

5 (a) $4a + 2b$ (b) $12a$ (c) $a + 6b + c$

6 (a) $\$(7y + 2p)$ (b) $\$(ty + 4p)$

7 (a) $\left(2a + \dfrac{b}{2}\right)$ km   (b) $\dfrac{1}{5}(4a + b)$ km/h

10.4

1 (b) $9y$ (c) $5x - 2y$ (d) $3x + 4y$

   (e) $11x + 2y$ (f) $4x - 6y$ (g) $x + y - 3z$

   (h) $3x - y - 6z$ (i) $2x - 6y + 1$ (j) $1 - x - 2y + 7z$

2 (a) a^6 (b) $a \times a$ (c) a^7 (d) a^7 (e) a^8; a^{m+n}

3 (a) a^3 (b) a^2 (c) a^4 (d) a^3 (e) a; a^{m-n}

4 (a) a^{13} (b) b^{12} (c) a^{15} (d) b^9 (e) a^4

   (f) b^6

5 (a) $6a^7$ (b) $\dfrac{7}{2}bc$ (c) $\dfrac{12}{5}\dfrac{ab^3}{c^2}$

10.5

1 (a) 351   (b) 896

2 **(b)** $3x + 15$ **(c)** $12 - 18x$ **(d)** $12x - 6y$
 (e) $4x^2 - 4xy$ **(f)** $6x^3 - 3x^2y$ **(g)** $4xy - xy^3$

3 **(b)** $3(x + 2y)$ **(c)** $7(x + 3)$ **(d)** $6(1 - 3y)$
 (e) $3(x + 2 + 3y)$ **(f)** $y(y - 1)$ **(g)** $xy(3x + 1 - 4y)$

4 **(a)** $5x + 5y$ **(b)** $11x - 7y$ **(c)** $9x - 22y$
 (d) $6x - 15$ **(e)** $24x^2 - 9x^2y$ **(f)** $x^2y - 4xy^2$

5 **(a)** $x^2 + 5x + 6$ **(b)** $x^2 + 5x + 5$

10.6

1 **(b)** 13 **(c)** 4 **(d)** 32 **(e)** 4 **(f)** 6
 (g) 4 **(h)** 7 **(i)** $11\frac{1}{2}$

2 **(a)** 2 **(b)** 9 **(c)** 5 **(d)** 2 **(e)** 7
 (f) 7 **(g)** 4 **(h)** 3 **(i)** 8

3 **(a)** 2 **(b)** 2 **(c)** 1 **(d)** 8 **(e)** 2
 (f) $1\frac{1}{3}$ **(g)** $\frac{2}{5}$ **(h)** 1 **(i)** $1\frac{1}{4}$

4 **(a)** 2 **(b)** 3 **(c)** 14 **(d)** 1 **(e)** $1\frac{17}{20}$
 (f) 1 **(h)** 22 **(i)** 29

10.7

1 19 **2** 55, 56 **3** 12 cm
4 $75 **5** 230 **6** 5

10.8

1 **(a)** $x = \dfrac{y - c}{2}$ **(b)** $x = \dfrac{yc - b}{a}$ **(c)** $x = \dfrac{y + d}{a} - b$
 (d) $x = \sqrt{\dfrac{3y}{2a}}$ **(e)** $x = \sqrt{\dfrac{y}{\pi h}}$

10.9

1 **(b)** $x > 5$ **(c)** $x < 4$ **(d)** $x < 5$
 (e) $x > 2\frac{4}{7}$ **(f)** $x < 9$

3 **(a)** $x < 1$ **(b)** $x \geqslant 2$ **(c)** $x \leqslant -2$

4 **(a)** $x < 4$ **(b)** $x > 8$ **(c)** $x < 4$ **(d)** $x > 9$
 (e) $x > 3$ **(f)** $x < 8$ **(g)** $x \geqslant 26$ **(h)** $x \leqslant -1\frac{1}{2}$

5 $w < 30$ m **6** **(a)** $2w + 2(w + 5) < 30$ **(b)** $w < 5$ cm

7 **(a)** $4r + 5(20 - r) \leqslant 90$ **(b)** 8

11.1

1 **(a)** 8 **(b)** 10 **(c)** 7
4 **(a)** 12 **(b)** 8

11.2

2 **(a)** 90 cm³ **(b)** 32 cm³ **(c)** 106.9 cm³
4 **(a)** 512 cm³ **(b)** 4096 cm³ **(c)** 8

11.3

1 **(a)** 12 cm², 60 cm³ **(b)** 4 cm², 48 cm³
 (c) 17.1 cm², 129.96 cm³

2 **(a)** 16 cm², 160 cm³ **(b)** 17.5 cm², 140 cm³
 (c) 28 cm², 280 cm³

3 **(a)** 113.04 cm², 904.32 cm³ **(b)** 12.56 cm², 125.6 cm³
 (c) 47.76 cm², 444.16 cm³

11.4

2 **(a)** 10 litres **(b)** 35 litres **(c)** 0.8 litres **(d)** 0.125 litres
3 **(a)** 2 m³ **(b)** 2 000 000 cm³ **(c)** 2000 litres

11.5

1 **(a)** 180 cm² **(b)** 250.32 cm²
2 **(a)** 216 cm³ **(b)** 86.64 cm³
3 **(a)** 336 cm² **(b)** 828 cm² **(c)** 81.6 cm²
4 **(a)** 552.64 cm² **(b)** 395.64 cm²
5 **(a)** 78.5 cm² **(b)** 471 cm² **(c)** 628 cm²
6 **(a)** 1840 cm² **(b)** yes

12.3

1 **(a)** $\frac{1}{4}$ **(b)** $\frac{13}{20}$ **(c)** $\frac{4}{5}$ **(d)** $\frac{17}{50}$ **(e)** $\frac{4}{25}$ **(f)** $\frac{7}{8}$
2 **(b)** 60% **(c)** 55% **(d)** 12%
 (e) 25% **(f)** 37.5%
4 **(b)** $30.50 **(c)** $600 **(d)** $3
 (e) $37.80 **(f)** $14.70

12.4

1 **(a)** $18 **(b)** $54 **(c)** $144 **(d)** $744
2 **(a)** $320 **(b)** $20 **(c)** $60
3 **(a)** $80 **(b)** $9600 **(c)** $1254
4 5 years **5** 5%

12.5

1 **(a)** $20 **(b)** $1020 **(c)** $20.40 **(d)** $40.40
3 **(a)** $1224 **(b)** $1845 **(c)** $1224.16
4 **(a)** $2496 **(b)** $104

12.6

1 **(a)** $18, $138 **(b)** $675, $5175
4 **(a)** **(i)** $60 000 **(ii)** $18 000 **(iii)** $82 000
 (b) **(i)** $0 **(ii)** $0

12.7

1 **(a)** $500, $9600, $10 100 **(b)** $300, $6000, $6300
2 **(a)** **(i)** $560, $7200, $7760 **(ii)** $105, $2080, $2185
 (b) **(i)** $2160 **(ii)** $85
3 $2320

Multiple choice 4

1 B	2 C	3 A	4 B	5 C	6 A	7 D
8 D	9 C	10 C	11 C	12 C	13 D	14 B
15 C	16 D	17 D	18 A	19 C	20 D	

Checklist - I can do it!